D0627905

JOSEPH ROTH

Job

The Story of a Simple Man

Translated from the German
and with an afterword by Ross Benjamin

archipelago books

Library of Congress Cataloging-in-Publication Data
Roth, Joseph, 1894–1939.
[Hiob, Roman eines einfachen Mannes. English]
Job, the story of a simple man / Joseph Roth ; translated from the
German by Ross Benjamin. – 1st Archipelago Books ed.
p. cm.
ISBN 978-0-9826246-3-0
I. Benjamin, Ross. II. Title.
PT2635.084H513 2010   833'.912 – dc22
2010038453

Archipelago Books
232 Third St. #A111
Brooklyn, NY 11215
www.archipelagobooks.org

Distributed by Consortium Book Sales and Distribution
www.cbsd.com

Cover art: Marc Chagall
Cover design: David Bullen

This publication was made possible by the generous support of Lannan
Foundation, The National Endowment for the Arts, and the New York
State Council on the Arts, a state agency.

Manufactured at Thomson-Shore, Inc. in Dexter, Michigan
Visit Thomson-Shore on the web at www.thomsonshore.com

Job

Part One

I

Many years ago there lived in Zuchnow a man named Mendel Singer. He was pious, God-fearing and ordinary, an entirely everyday Jew. He practiced the modest profession of a teacher. In his house, which consisted of only a roomy kitchen, he imparted to children knowledge of the Bible. He taught with genuine enthusiasm and without spectacular success. Hundreds of thousands before him had lived and taught as he did.

As insignificant as his nature was his pale face. A full beard of ordinary black framed it completely. His mouth was hidden by the beard. His eyes were large, black, languid and half veiled by heavy lids. On his head sat a cap of black silk rep, a material out of which unfashionable and cheap ties are sometimes made. His body was wrapped in a customary half-long Jewish caftan, the skirts of which fluttered when Mendel Singer rushed through the street, knocking with a hard regular wing beat against the shafts of his high leather boots.

Singer seemed to have little time and nothing but pressing goals. Certainly his life was always hard and at times even a torment. He had a wife and three children to clothe and feed. (She was pregnant with a fourth.) God had bestowed fertility on his loins, equanimity on his heart and poverty on his hands. They had no gold to weigh and no banknotes to count. Still, his life ran steadily along like a poor little brook between sparse banks. Each morning Mendel thanked God for his sleep, for his awakening and for the dawning day. When the sun went down, he prayed once more. When the first stars began to sparkle, he prayed a third time. And before he lay down to sleep, he whispered a hasty prayer with weary but zealous lips. His sleep was dreamless. His conscience was clear. His soul was chaste. He had nothing to regret and there was nothing he would have coveted. He loved his wife and delighted in her flesh. With healthy hunger he swiftly consumed his meals. His two small sons, Jonas and Shemariah, he beat when they were disobedient. But the youngest, his daughter Miriam, he caressed often. She had his black hair and his black, languid and gentle eyes. Her limbs were delicate, her joints fragile. A young gazelle.

He taught twelve six-year-old pupils reading and recitation of the Bible. Every Friday each of the twelve brought him twenty kopecks. This was Mendel Singer's only income. He was only thirty years old. But his prospects of earning more were slim, perhaps nonexistent. When the pupils grew older, they moved on to other, wiser teachers. Life became more expensive from year to year. The harvests were poorer and poorer. The carrots decreased, the eggs became hollow, the potatoes frozen, the soups watery, the carp thin and the pike short, the ducks meager, the geese tough, and the chickens nothing.

Thus sounded the laments of Deborah, Mendel Singer's wife. She was a woman, occasionally something got into her. She stole glances at the property of the wealthy and envied merchants their profits. Mendel Singer was much too lowly in her eyes. She reproached him for the children, her pregnancy, the rising prices, his low fees and often even for the bad weather. On Friday she scrubbed the floor until it turned yellow as saffron. Her broad shoulders jerked up and down in a regular rhythm, her strong hands rubbed vigorously every single floorboard, and her nails dug into the gaps and hollow spaces between the boards and scraped out black grime, which breaking waves from the bucket completely obliterated. Like a broad, mighty and mobile mountain, she crawled through the bare, blue-washed room. Outside the door she aired the furniture, the brown wooden bed, the sacks of straw, a planed-down table, two long and narrow benches, horizontal boards, each of them nailed to two vertical ones. As soon as the first twilight breathed on the window, Deborah lit the candles in candlesticks made of nickel silver, covered her face with her hands and prayed. Her husband came home in silky black, the floor shone up at him, yellow as melted sun, his face shimmered whiter than usual, and blacker than on weekdays his beard darkened. He sat down, sang a little song, then the parents and children slurped the hot soup, smiled at the plates and spoke not a word. Warmth rose in the room. It swarmed from the pots, the bowls, the bodies. The cheap candles in the nickel silver candlesticks couldn't stand it, they began to bend. Stearin dripped on the brick-red and blue checkered tablecloth and encrusted in no time. The window was flung open, the candles braced up and burned peacefully to their end. The children lay down on the sacks of straw near the stove, the parents remained sitting and gazed with troubled solemnity into the last little blue flames, which shot up jaggedly out of the cavities of the candlesticks and, gently undulating, sank back, a fountain of fire. The stearin smoldered, thin blue threads of smoke drifted upward to the ceiling from the charred remains of the wick. "Ah!" sighed the woman. "Don't sigh!" Mendel Singer admonished. They fell silent. "Let's sleep, Deborah!" he commanded. And they began to murmur a bedtime prayer.

At the end of each week the Sabbath commenced thus, with silence, candles and song. Twenty-four hours later it was submerged in the night that led the gray procession of weekdays, a round dance of tribulation. On a hot midsummer day, in the fourth hour of the afternoon, Deborah gave birth. Her first cries pierced the singsong of the twelve studying children. They all went home. Seven days of vacation began. Mendel got a new child, a fourth, a boy. Eight days later he was circumcised and named Menuchim.

Menuchim had no cradle. He hung in a wicker basket in the middle of the room, fastened with four ropes to a hook in the ceiling like a chandelier. From time to time Mendel Singer tapped with a gentle, not loveless finger on the hanging basket, which immediately began to rock. Occasionally, this motion calmed the infant. But sometimes nothing helped against his desire to whimper and scream. His voice croaked over the holy sentences of the Bible. Deborah climbed onto a stool and took the infant down. White, swollen and colossal, her bosom poured from her open blouse and drew the glances of the boys overpoweringly. Deborah seemed to suckle all present. Her own three older children surrounded her, jealous and desirous. Silence fell. They heard the infant's smacking.

The days stretched into weeks, the weeks grew into months, twelve months made a year. Menuchim still drank his mother's milk, a thin, clear milk. She couldn't wean him. In the thirteenth month of his life he began to make faces and groan like an animal, to breathe in racing haste and gasp in a previously unknown way. His large head hung heavy as a pumpkin on his thin neck. His broad brow folded and furrowed all over like a crumpled parchment. His legs were curved and lifeless like two wooden bows. His scrawny little arms wriggled and twitched. His mouth stammered ridiculous sounds. When he had an attack, he was taken out of the cradle and shaken well, until his face turned bluish and he nearly lost his breath. Then he recovered slowly. Brewed tea (in several little bags) was laid on his meager chest and coltsfoot was wrapped around his thin neck. "It's nothing," said his father, "it comes from growing." "Sons take after their mother's brothers.

My brother had it for five years!" said his mother. "He'll grow out of it!" said the others. Until one day smallpox broke out in the town, the authorities prescribed vaccinations, and the doctors penetrated into the houses of the Jews. Some hid. But Mendel Singer, the righteous, fled no divine punishment. Even the vaccination he awaited calmly.

It was a hot sunny morning when the commission came through Mendel's street. The last in the row of Jewish houses was Mendel's house. With a police officer, who was carrying a large book under his arm, Dr. Soltysiuk walked with broad strides, a fluttering blonde mustache on his brown face, a gold-rimmed pince-nez on his reddened nose, in creaking yellow leather leggings, and his coat hanging casually over his blue *rubashka* due to the heat so that the sleeves looked like another pair of arms, which seemed equally poised to perform vaccinations: thus came Dr. Soltysiuk into the street of the Jews. Toward him resounded the wailing of women and the howling of children who had not been able to hide. The police officer hauled women and children out of deep cellars and down from high attics, out of tiny closets and large straw baskets. The sun brooded, the doctor sweated. He had no less than one hundred and seventy-six Jews to vaccinate. For each one who had escaped and could not be reached he thanked God inwardly. When he came to the fourth of the little blue-washed houses, he beckoned to the police officer to stop searching so zealously. The farther the doctor went, the louder the screaming swelled. It wafted along before his strides. The howls of those who were still afraid joined the curses of the already vaccinated. Weary and completely disconcerted, he sank down with a heavy groan on the bench in Mendel's kitchen and asked for a glass of water. His glance fell on little Menuchim, he lifted up the cripple and said: "He will be an epileptic." He poured fear into the father's heart. "All children have spasms," the mother objected. "It's not that," declared the doctor. "But I might be able to cure him. There's life in his eyes."

He wanted to take the little one to the hospital at once. Deborah was ready. "They'll cure him for free," she said. But Mendel replied: "Be quiet, Deborah! No doctor can cure him if God doesn't will it. Shall he grow up among Russian children? Hear not one holy word? Eat milk with meat and chickens fried in butter, as they are served in the hospital? We are poor, but I will not sell Menuchim's soul just because he can be cured for free. One is not healed in strange hospitals." Like a hero Mendel held out his scrawny white arm for the vaccination. But he did not give Menuchim away. He resolved to beg God's help for his youngest and to fast twice a week, Monday and Thursday. Deborah decided to make pilgrimages to the cemetery and appeal to the bones of the ancestors to intercede with the almighty. Thus would Menuchim become healthy and not an epileptic.

Nonetheless, after the hour of the vaccination, fear hung over the house of Mendel Singer like a monster, and sorrow blew through their hearts like a constant hot and biting wind. Deborah could sigh, and her husband did not reprimand her. Longer than usual she held her head buried in her hands when she prayed, as if she were creating her own nights, to bury her fear in them, and her own darknesses, so as to find grace in them. For she believed, as it was written, that God's light shone in the dimnesses and his goodness illuminated the blackness. But Menuchim's attacks did not cease. The older children grew and grew, their health clamored evilly in their mother's ears like an enemy of Menuchim, the invalid. It was as if the healthy children drew strength from the sick one, and Deborah hated their shouting, their red cheeks, their straight limbs. She made pilgrimages to the cemetery through rain and sun. She struck her head against the mossy sandstone that grew from the bones of her fathers and mothers. She invoked the dead, whose silent consoling replies she believed she heard. On the way home she trembled with the hope of finding her son healthy. She neglected her duty at the stove, the soup boiled over, the clay pots cracked, the pans rusted, the greenish shimmering glasses shattered with a harsh crash, the chimney of the petroleum lamp was darkened with soot, the wick was charred to a miserable stub, the dirt of many soles and many weeks coated the floorboards, the lard melted away in the pot, the withered buttons fell from the children's shirts like leaves before the winter.

One day, a week before the high holy days (the summer had turned into rain, and the rain wanted to turn into snow), Deborah packed her son in the basket, laid wool blankets over him, placed him on the coachman Sameshkin's cart, and traveled to Kluczýsk, where the rabbi lived. The board seat lay loosely on the straw and slid with every movement of the wagon. Deborah held it down with only her body weight, it was alive, it wanted to jump. The narrow winding road was covered with silver-gray mud in which the high boots of the passersby and the bottom halves of the wheels sank. Rain veiled the fields, scattered the smoke over the isolated huts, ground with endless, fine patience everything solid that it struck, the limestone that here and there grew like a white tooth out of the black earth, the sawed-up logs on the sides of the road, the fragrant boards piled in front of the entrance to the sawmill, also Deborah's headscarf and the wool blankets under which Menuchim lay buried. Not one little drop should wet him. Deborah reckoned that she still had four hours to travel; if the rain didn't cease, she would have to stop at the inn and dry the blankets, drink tea and eat the poppy-seed pretzels she had brought along, which were now soggy too. That could cost five kopecks, five kopecks with which one must not be careless. God showed understanding, it stopped raining. Above hasty wisps of clouds a dissolved sun paled for scarcely an hour; in a new deeper twilight it finally sank.

Black night had settled in Kluczýsk when Deborah arrived. Many helpless people had already come to see the rabbi. Kluczýsk consisted of a few thousand low straw and shingle-covered houses, a kilometer-wide marketplace that was like a dry lake wreathed with buildings. The carts that stood around in it were reminiscent of stranded wrecks; and they were lost, tiny and meaningless, in the circular expanse. The unhitched horses whinnied next to the carts and trod the sticky mud with tired, slapping hooves. Solitary men wandered with swaying yellow lanterns through the round night to fetch a forgotten blanket and some rattling dishes with provisions. All around, in the thousand little houses, the arrivals were taken in. They slept on plank-beds next to the residents' beds, the infirm, the misshapen, the lame, the mad, the idiotic, the heart-afflicted, the diabetic, who bore cancer in their bodies, whose eyes were contaminated with trachoma, women with infertile wombs, mothers with deformed children, men threatened by prison or military service, deserters who prayed for a successful escape, those given up on by doctors, cast out by mankind, maltreated by earthly justice, the troubled, the yearning, the starving and the satiated, deceivers and the honest, all, all, all . . . Deborah stayed with her husband's Kluczýsk relatives. She didn't sleep. She crouched all night beside Menuchim's basket in the corner next to the stove; dark was the room, dark was her heart. She no longer dared appeal to God, He seemed to her too high, too great, too remote, infinitely far beyond infinite heavens, she would have needed a ladder of a million prayers to reach even a hem of God's garment. She sought help from the dead, appealed to her parents, Menuchim's grandfather after whom the little one was named, then the patriarchs of the Jews, Abraham, Isaac and Jacob, the bones of Moses, and finally the matriarchs. Wherever support was possible she sent a sigh. She pounded on a hundred graves, on a hundred doors of paradise. For fear that she wouldn't reach the rabbi tomorrow because too many supplicants were there, she first prayed for the good fortune to make it there early, as if her son's recovery would then be child's play. Finally she saw through the cracks of the black window shutters a few pale streaks of morning. She rose quickly. She kindled the dry pine chips that lay on the stove, sought and found a pot, fetched the samovar from the table, threw in the burning chips, poured in coal, held the urn by both handles, bent down and blew into it so that the sparks flew out and crackled about her face. It was as if she were acting in accordance with a mysterious rite. Soon the water boiled, soon the tea brewed, the family rose, they sat down in front of the earthen brown dishes and drank. Then Deborah lifted her son out of the basket. He whimpered. She kissed him rapidly and many times, with a frantic tenderness, her moist lips smacked on the gray face, the scrawny little hands, the crooked thighs, the bloated belly of the little one, it was as if she were striking the child with her loving motherly mouth. Then she wrapped him up, tied a cord around the package, and hung her son around her neck so that her hands would be free. She wanted to clear a way through the throng in front of the rabbi's door.

With a sharp scream she plunged into the waiting crowd, with cruel fists she forced apart the weak, no one could stop her. Whoever, struck by her hand and pushed away, looked after her so as to send her back was blinded by the burning pain in her face, by her open red mouth, from which a scorching breath seemed to stream, by the crystal gleam of her large rolling tears, by her cheeks, ablaze in red flames, by the thick blue veins on her craned neck, in which the cries gathered before they broke out. Like a torch Deborah wafted along. With a single shrill cry, in the wake of which the terrible silence of a whole dead world ensued, Deborah finally reached the rabbi's door and fell down before it, the latch in her outstretched right hand. With her left she pounded against the brown wood. Menuchim grazed the ground in front of her.

Someone opened the door. The rabbi stood at the window, his back to her, a thin black line. Suddenly he turned around. She remained at the threshold, she presented her son on both arms, as one offers a sacrifice. She caught a glimmer from the man's pale face, which seemed to be one with his white beard. She had planned to look into the holy man's eyes so as to convince herself that powerful goodness truly lived in them. But now that she stood there, a lake of tears lay before her gaze, and she saw the man behind a white wave of water and salt. He raised his hand, she thought she discerned two scrawny fingers, instruments of blessing. But very close to her she heard the voice of the rabbi, though he only whispered:

"Menuchim, Mendel's son, will grow healthy. There will not be many of his like in Israel. Pain will make him wise, ugliness kind, bitterness gentle, and illness strong. His eyes will be far and deep, his ears clear and full of echoes. His mouth will be silent, but when he will open his lips, they will herald good things. Have no fear and go home!"

"When, when, when will he be healthy?" Deborah whispered.

"After long years," said the rabbi, "but don't question me further, I have no time and know nothing more. Do not leave your son, even if he is a great burden to you, do not give him away, he comes from you just as a healthy child does. And go!"

Outside the people cleared the way for her. Her cheeks were pale, her eyes dry, her lips slightly opened, as if she were breathing pure hope. Grace in her heart, she returned home.

II

When Deborah returned home, she found her husband at the stove. Grudgingly he tended the fire, the pot, the wooden spoons. His upright mind was directed toward the simple earthly things and tolerated no miracle within range of his eyes. He smiled at his wife's faith in the rabbi. His simple piety required no mediating power between God and man. "Menuchim will grow healthy, but it will take a long time!" With these words Deborah entered the house. "It will take a long time!" repeated Mendel like an evil echo. With a sigh Deborah hung the basket from the ceiling again. The three older children came from their play. They set upon the basket, which they had missed for a few days, and swung it forcefully. Mendel Singer seized his sons, Jonas and Shemariah, with both hands. Miriam, the girl, fled to her mother. Mendel pinched his sons' ears. They howled out. He unbuckled his belt and swung it through the air. As if the leather were part of his body, as if it were the natural continuation of his hand, Mendel Singer felt each slapping lash that struck his sons' backs. An uncanny roar broke out in his head. His wife's warning cries fell into his own noise and died away meaninglessly in it. It was as if glasses of water were being poured into a turbulent sea. He didn't feel where he stood. He whirled the swinging, cracking belt around, struck the walls, the table, the benches, and didn't know whether the missed lashes pleased him more or the successful ones. Finally the wall clock struck three, the hour in which the pupils gathered in the afternoon. With an empty stomach – for he had not eaten anything – and the choking agitation still in his throat, Mendel began to recite word after word, sentence upon sentence from the Bible. The bright choir of children's voices repeated word after word, sentence after sentence, it was as if the Bible were being tolled by many bells. Like bells the students' upper bodies swung forward and back, while above their heads Menuchim's basket swung in almost the same rhythm. Today Mendel's sons participated in the lesson. Their father's rage dissipated, cooled down, died out, because they were more advanced than the others in chanting recitation. To test them, he left the room. The choir of children sounded on, led by the voices of his sons. He could rely on them.

Jonas, the older, was strong as a bear, Shemariah, the younger, was sly as a fox. Stamping, Jonas trudged along, with his head bent forward, with hanging hands, bursting cheeks, eternal hunger, curly hair that grew profusely over the edges of his cap. Gentle and almost creeping, with a sharp profile, with constantly alert, bright eyes, thin arms, hands buried in his pockets, his brother Shemariah followed him. A quarrel never broke out between them, they were too distant from each other, their realms and possessions were separate, they had formed a pact. Out of tin cans, matchboxes, pottery fragments, horns, willow twigs, Shemariah made wonderful things. Jonas could have blown them over and destroyed them with his strong breath. But he admired his brother's delicate adroitness. His little black eyes flashed like tiny sparks between his cheeks, curious and cheerful.

A few days after her return, Deborah believed that the time had come to unfasten Menuchim's basket from the ceiling. Not without solemnity she handed the little one over to the older children. "You will take him walking!" said Deborah. "When he gets tired, you will carry him. Do not drop him, God forbid! The holy man has said he will grow healthy. Do him no harm." From that point on began the children's torment.

They dragged Menuchim through the town like a misfortune, they left him unattended, they dropped him. They found it hard to endure the scorn of the other children their age, who followed them when they took Menuchim walking. The little one had to be held between two of them. He didn't put one foot in front of the other like a person. His legs wobbled like two broken wheels, he stopped, he collapsed. Finally Jonas and Shemariah left him unattended. They put him in a corner, in a sack. There he played with dog excrement, horse dung, pebbles. He devoured everything. He scratched the lime from the walls and stuffed his mouth full, then coughed and turned blue in the face. A piece of rubbish, he lay in the corner. Sometimes he started to cry. The boys sent Miriam to console him. Delicate, coquettish, with thin skipping legs, an ugly and hateful disgust in her heart, she approached her ridiculous brother. The tenderness with which she stroked his ash-gray wrinkled face had something murderous about it. She looked around carefully, to the right and to the left, and then she pinched her brother's thighs. He howled out, neighbors looked out their windows. She contorted her face into a weepy grimace. Everyone took pity on her and asked what was wrong.

One rainy day in summer the children dragged Menuchim out of the house and stuck him in a tub in which rainwater had been collecting for half a year, worms were floating around, fruit scraps and moldy bread crusts. They held him by his crooked legs and plunged his broad gray head a dozen times into the water. Then they pulled him out, with pounding hearts, red cheeks, in the joyful and horrible expectation of holding a corpse. But Menuchim lived. His breath rattled, he spat up the water, the worms, the moldy bread, the fruit scraps, and lived. Nothing happened to him. Then the children carried him silently and anxiously back into the house. A great fear before God's little finger, which had just waved very softly, seized the two boys and the girl. All day they didn't speak to one another. Their tongues were stuck to the roofs of their mouths, their lips opened to form a word, but no sound took shape in their throats. It stopped raining, the sun appeared, rivulets flowed cheerfully along the edges of the streets. It would have been time to launch paper boats and watch them float toward the canal. But nothing at all happened. The children crept back into the house like dogs. All afternoon they waited for Menuchim's death. Menuchim didn't die.

Menuchim didn't die, he stayed alive, a powerful cripple. From that point on, Deborah's womb was dry and infertile. Menuchim was the last, failed fruit of her body, it was as if her womb were refusing to bring forth still more misfortune. In fleeting moments she embraced her husband. They were brief as lightning, dry lightning on the distant summer horizon. Long, cruel and sleepless were Deborah's nights. A wall of cold glass separated her from her husband. Her breasts withered, her body swelled like a mockery of her infertility, her thighs became heavy, and lead clung to her feet.

One morning in summer she awoke earlier than Mendel. A chirping sparrow on the windowsill had roused her. Its whistle was still in her ear, the memory of something dreamed, something happy, like the voice of a sunbeam. The early warm dawn penetrated the pores and cracks of the wooden window shutters, and even though the edges of the furniture still dissolved in the shadow of the night, Deborah's eyes were already clear, her thoughts hard, her heart cool. She cast a glance at the sleeping man and discovered the first white hairs in his black beard. He cleared his throat in his sleep. He snored. Quickly she leaped in front of the murky mirror. She ran her cold, combing fingers through her thin hair, pulled one strand after another over her forehead, and searched for white hairs. She thought she found one, grasped it with the hard pincers of two fingers, and tore it out. Then she opened her shirt before the mirror. She saw her sagging breasts, lifted them, let them fall, stroked her hand over her hollow and yet bulging body, saw the blue branching veins on her thighs, and decided to go back to bed. She turned around, and her frightened gaze met the open eye of her husband. "What are you looking at?" she cried. He didn't answer. It was as if the open eye did not belong to him, for he himself was still asleep. It had opened independently of him. It had become curious on its own. The white of the eye seemed whiter than usual. The pupil was tiny. The eye reminded Deborah of a frozen lake with a black spot in it. It could scarcely have been open for a minute, but to Deborah that minute felt like a decade. Mendel's eye closed again. He continued to breathe quietly, he was asleep, without a doubt. A distant trilling of a million larks arose outside, above the house, below the heavens. The dawning heat of the young day already penetrated the morning darkness of the room. Soon the clock would strike six, the hour in which Mendel Singer usually got up. Deborah didn't move. She remained where she had stood when she had turned to the bed, the mirror at her back. Never before had she stood thus, listening, without purpose, without need, without curiosity, without desire. She was waiting for nothing at all. But it seemed to her that she must have been waiting for something special. All her senses were awake as never before, and a few unknown, new senses were aroused in support of the old ones. She saw, heard, felt a thousand times over. And nothing at all happened. Only a summer morning dawned, only larks trilled in the unreachable distance, only sunbeams forced their way through the cracks in the shutters with hot power, and the broad shadows at the edges of the furniture grew narrower and narrower, and the clock ticked and prepared to strike six, and the man breathed. Soundlessly the children lay in the corner next to the stove, visible to Deborah but far away, as if in another room. Nothing at all happened. Yet infinite things seemed to want to happen. The clock struck like a release. Mendel Singer awoke, sat up straight in bed and stared in astonishment at his wife. "Why aren't you in bed?" he asked, rubbing his eyes. He coughed and spat. Nothing at all about his words or his demeanor betrayed that his left eye had been open and had gazed on its own. Perhaps he didn't recall, or perhaps Deborah had been mistaken.

From that day on, the desire ceased between Mendel Singer and his wife. Like two people of the same sex they lay down, slept through the nights, awoke in the morning. They felt ashamed before each other and were silent, as in the first days of their marriage. Shame was at the beginning of their desire, and at the end of their desire was shame too.

Then it too was overcome. They talked again, their eyes no longer avoided each other, their faces and their bodies aged in the same rhythm, like the faces and bodies of twins. The summer was languid and stifling and poor in rain. Door and window stood open. The children were rarely at home. Outside they grew quickly, invigorated by the sun.

Even Menuchim grew. Though his legs remained curved, they were unquestionably longer. His upper body stretched out too. Suddenly, one morning, he emitted a previously unheard, shrill cry. Then he was silent. Awhile later he said clearly and audibly: "Mama."

Deborah flung herself upon him, and from her eyes, which had long been dry, flowed tears, hot, strong, large, salty, painful and sweet. "Say: Mama!" "Mama," repeated the little one. A dozen times he repeated the word. A hundred times Deborah repeated it. Her prayers had not been in vain. Menuchim spoke. And this one word of the deformed child was sublime as a revelation, mighty as thunder, warm as love, gracious as heaven, wide as the earth, fertile as a field, sweet as a sweet fruit. It was more than the health of the healthy children. It meant that Menuchim would be strong and big, wise and kind, as the words of the blessing had said.

However: no other comprehensible sounds came from Menuchim's throat. For a long time this one word that he had produced after such terrible silence meant food and drink, sleep and love, pleasure and pain, heaven and earth. Though he said only this word at every occasion, he seemed to his mother Deborah as eloquent as a preacher and as rich in expression as a poet. She understood every word that was hidden in this one. She neglected the older children. She turned away from them. She had but one son, her only son: Menuchim.

III

Perhaps blessings need a longer time for their fulfillment than curses. Ten years had passed since Menuchim had spoken his first and only word. He could still say nothing else.

Sometimes, when Deborah was alone in the house with her sick son, she bolted the door, sat down next to Menuchim on the floor, and stared into the little one's face. She remembered the frightful day in summer when the countess had driven up to the church. Deborah sees the open portal of the church. A golden glow of a thousand candles, of colorful pictures wreathed with light, of three priests in vestments standing deep and far at the altar, with black beards and white hovering hands, penetrates the white sunlit dusty square. Deborah is in her third month, Menuchim is stirring in her body, she is holding little, delicate Miriam firmly by the hand. Suddenly shouts ring out. They drown out the singing of the worshipers in the church. The staccato clatter of horses can be heard, a cloud of dust whirls up, the dark blue equipage of the countess stops in front of the church. The peasant children cheer. The beggars on the steps hobble toward the carriage to kiss the countess's hand. All of a sudden Miriam breaks free. In no time she has disappeared. Deborah trembles, she's freezing, in the midst of the heat. Where is Miriam? She asks every peasant child. The countess has climbed out. Deborah comes very close to the carriage. The coachman with the silver buttons on his dark blue livery sits so high that he can look out over everything. "Did you see the little black girl running?" asks Deborah, craning her neck, her eyes blinded by the brightness of the sun and the liveried man. The coachman points with his white-gloved left hand into the church. Miriam has run in there. Deborah considers for a moment, then plunges into the church, into the golden glow, into the full singing, into the thunder of the organ. In the entrance stands Miriam. Deborah seizes the child, drags her into the square, runs down the white-hot steps, flees as if from a fire. She wants to strike the child, but she is afraid.

She runs, pulling the child behind her, into a side street. Now she is calmer. "You must tell your father nothing of this," she gasps. "Do you hear, Miriam?"

From this day on, Deborah knows that a misfortune is approaching. She is carrying a misfortune in her womb. She knows it and is silent. She unbolts the door, there's a knock, Mendel is home.

His beard is prematurely gray. Prematurely withered were also Deborah's face, body and hands. Strong and slow as a bear was the oldest son Jonas, sly and quick as a fox the younger son Shemariah, coquettish and thoughtless as a gazelle the sister

Miriam. When she glided through the streets to run errands, svelte and thin, a shimmering shadow, a brown face, a big red mouth, a golden-yellow shawl knotted under her chin in two fluttering wings, and the two old eyes in the midst of the brown youth of her face, she caught the attention of the officers of the garrison and stuck in their carefree, pleasure-craving minds. Occasionally some of them chased her. She noticed nothing about her hunters but what she could take in directly through the outer gates of her senses: a silver clanking and rattling of spurs and weapons, an enveloping fragrance of pomade and shaving soap, a glaring shimmer of golden buttons, silver braids and blood-red reins of Russian leather. It was little, it was enough. Just behind the outer gates of Miriam's senses lurked curiosity, the sister of youth, the herald of desire. In sweet and hot fear the girl fled her pursuers. Only so as to savor the painful exciting pleasure of the fear, she fled through several side streets, many minutes longer. She fled by a roundabout route. Only so as to be able to flee again, Miriam left the house more often than necessary. On street corners she stopped and cast glances back, bait for the hunters. These were Miriam's only pleasures. Even if there had been someone who understood her, her mouth would have remained closed. For pleasures are stronger so long as they remain secret.

Miriam did not yet know what a threatening relationship she would have to the strange and terrible world of the military and how heavy the fates were that were already beginning to gather over the heads of Mendel Singer, his wife and his children. For

Jonas and Shemariah were already at the age when according to the law they were supposed to become soldiers and according to the tradition of their fathers they had to escape from service. A gracious and provident God had given other youths a physical affliction that didn't disable them much and protected them from the evil. Some were one-eyed, some limped, this one had a hernia, that one jerked his arms and legs for no reason, several had weak lungs, others weak hearts, one was hard of hearing and another stuttered and a third quite simply had general physical weakness. But in Mendel Singer's family it seemed as if little Menuchim had taken on himself the sum total of human agonies, which a kind nature might otherwise have distributed little by little among all the members. Mendel's older sons were healthy, no defect could be discovered on their bodies, and they had to begin to torment themselves, to fast and drink black coffee and hope for at least a temporary heart condition, though the war against Japan was already over.

And thus began their torments. They didn't eat, they didn't sleep, they staggered weak and trembling through days and nights. Their eyes were reddened and swollen, their necks thin, and their heads heavy. Deborah loved them again. To pray for the older sons, she again made pilgrimages to the cemetery. This time she prayed for an illness for Jonas and Shemariah, as she had once begged for Menuchim's health. The military rose before her troubled eyes like a heavy mountain of smooth iron and clanking torture. Corpses she saw, nothing but corpses. High and gleaming, his spurred feet in red blood, sat the Tsar, waiting for the sacrifice of her sons. They went on maneuvers, this alone was for her already the greatest terror, she didn't even think of a new war. She was angry with her husband. Mendel Singer, what was he? A teacher, a stupid teacher of stupid children. She'd had something else in mind when she was still a young girl. Mendel Singer meanwhile found the distress no easier to bear than his wife did. On the Sabbath in the synagogue, when the legally prescribed prayer for the Tsar was held, Mendel thought about his sons' imminent future. He could already see them in the detested khaki uniforms of fresh recruits. They ate pork and were lashed by officers with riding whips. They carried rifles and bayonets. He often sighed for no conceivable reason, in the midst of praying, in the midst of instruction, in the midst of silence. Even strangers gave him concerned looks. About his sick son no one had ever asked him, but about his healthy sons everyone inquired.

On the twenty-sixth of March, finally, the two brothers traveled to Targi. Both drew lots. Both were in perfect health. Both were taken.

They were allowed to spend one more summer at home. In autumn they had to report for duty. On a Wednesday they became soldiers. On Sunday they returned home.

On Sunday they returned home, equipped with complimentary tickets from the state. Already they were traveling at the expense of the Tsar. Many of their kind rode with them. It was a slow train. They sat on wooden benches among peasants. The peasants sang and were drunk. All of them smoked black tobacco, with the smoke of which a distant memory of sweat mingled its scent. All told one another stories. Jonas and Shemariah didn't separate from each other for an instant. It was their first railroad journey. Often they switched seats. Each of them wanted to sit by the window for a little while and look into the landscape. To Shemariah the world appeared tremendously vast. It was flat in Jonas's eyes, it bored him. The train ran smoothly through the flat land like a sleigh over snow. The fields lay in the windows. The colorful peasant women waved. Where they appeared in groups, the peasants in the car greeted them with resounding howls. Black, shy and anxious, the two Jews sat among them, pushed into the corner by the exuberance of the drunken peasants. "I'd like to be a peasant," Jonas suddenly said.

"Not I," replied Shemariah.

"I'd like to be a peasant," repeated Jonas, "I'd like to be drunk and sleep with the girls there."

"I want to be what I am," said Shemariah, "a Jew like my father Mendel Singer, not a soldier, and sober."

"I'm a little bit glad that I'm going to be a soldier," said Jonas.

"You'll experience your pleasures! I'd rather be a rich man and see life."

"What is life?"

"Life," declared Shemariah, "is to be seen in big cities. The trams run in the middle of the streets, all the shops are as big as our gendarmerie barracks, and the display windows are even bigger. I've seen postcards. You don't need a door to enter a shop, the windows reach down to your feet."

"Hey, why are you so gloomy?" a peasant suddenly cried from the opposite corner.

Jonas and Shemariah acted as if they hadn't heard or as if his question hadn't been directed at them. To pretend to be deaf when a peasant talked to them was in their blood. For a thousand years nothing good had ever come of it when a peasant asked and a Jew answered.

"Hey!" said the peasant, standing up.

Jonas and Shemariah stood up at the same time.

"Yes, I was speaking to you, Jews," said the peasant. "Have you had nothing to drink yet?"

"Already had our drink," said Shemariah.

"I haven't," said Jonas.

The peasant pulled out a bottle he'd been carrying on his breast under his jacket. It was warm and slippery and smelled more strongly of the peasant than of its contents. Jonas put it to his mouth. He bared his full blood-red lips, on both sides of the brown bottle his strong white teeth could be seen. Jonas drank and drank. He didn't feel his brother's light hand, which touched his sleeve admonishingly. With both hands, like a gigantic infant, he held the bottle. On his raised elbows, his shirt shimmered white through the worn thin material. Regularly, like a piston in a machine, his Adam's apple rose and sank under the skin of his neck. A soft muffled gurgle rumbled from his throat. Everyone watched as the Jew drank.

Jonas was finished. The empty bottle fell out of his hands and into his brother Shemariah's lap. He himself sank down after it, as if he had to take the same path. The peasant held out his hand, silently asking Shemariah for the bottle back. Then he caressed a little bit with his boot the broad shoulders of the sleeping Jonas.

They reached Podvorsk, where they had to get off. It was seven versts to Yurki, the brothers had to hike on foot, who knows whether someone would take them on a wagon along the way. All the travelers helped lift the heavy Jonas to his feet. Once he stood outside, he was sober again.

They hiked. It was night. They sensed the moon behind milky clouds. Scattered, irregularly contoured patches of earth darkened on the snow-covered fields like the mouths of craters. Spring seemed to waft from the woods. Jonas and Shemariah walked quickly on a narrow path. They heard the fine crackle of the thin brittle shell of ice under their boots. Their white round bundles they carried on sticks over their shoulders. A few times Shemariah tried to start a conversation with his brother. Jonas didn't reply. He felt ashamed because he had drunk and fallen down like a peasant. In the places where the path was so narrow that the two brothers could not walk side-by-side, Jonas let his younger brother go ahead. He preferred to have Shemariah walk in front of him.

When the path widened again, he slowed his pace in the hope that Shemariah would walk on without waiting for his brother. But it was as if the younger one feared losing the older. Since he'd seen that Jonas could be drunk, he no longer trusted him, doubted the older one's reason, felt responsible for him. Jonas surmised what his brother was feeling. A great senseless rage boiled in his heart. "Shemariah is ridiculous," thought Jonas. "He's thin as a ghost, he can't even hold the stick, he shoulders it again and again, the bundle is going to fall in the dirt." At the idea that Shemariah's white bundle could fall from the smooth stick into the black dirt of the road, Jonas laughed aloud. "What are you laughing at?" asked Shemariah. "At you!" answered Jonas. "I'd have more right to laugh at you," said Shemariah. Again they fell silent. The pine forest grew blackly toward them. From it, not from themselves, the silence seemed to come. From time to time a wind arose from an arbitrary direction, a homeless gust. A willow bush stirred in its sleep, branches cracked dryly, the clouds ran brightly across the sky. "So now we are soldiers!" Shemariah suddenly said. "That's right," said Jonas, "and what were we before? We have no profession. Should we become teachers like our father?" "Better than being a soldier!" said Shemariah. "I could become a merchant and go out into the world!" "Soldiers are world too, and I can't be a merchant," Jonas declared. "You're drunk!" "I'm as sober as you. I can drink and be sober. I can be a soldier and see the world. I'd like to be a peasant. That I tell you – and I'm not drunk . . . "

Shemariah shrugged his shoulders. They walked on. Toward morning they heard the cocks crowing from distant farms. "That must be Yurki," said Shemariah.

"No, it's Bytók!" said Jonas.

"Fine, Bytók!" said Shemariah.

A cart clattered and rattled around the next bend of the path. The morning was pale, as the night had been. No difference between moon and sun. Snow began to fall, soft, warm snow. Ravens took wing and cawed.

"Look at the birds," said Shemariah; only as a pretext to placate his brother.

"Those are ravens!" said Jonas. "Birds!" he mimicked mockingly.

"Fine!" said Shemariah. "Ravens!"

It really was Bytók. Another hour and they'd be home.

It snowed thicker and softer as the day progressed, as if the snow were coming from the rising sun. In a few minutes the whole country was white. Also the individual willows along the path and the scattered groups of birches among the fields, white, white, white. Only the two young striding Jews were black. They too were showered with snow, but on their backs it seemed to melt faster. Their long black coats fluttered. The skirts knocked with a hard regular beat against the shafts of the their high leather boots. The thicker it snowed, the faster they walked. Peasants coming toward them walked very slowly, with bent knees, they turned white, on their broad shoulders the snow lay as on thick branches, at once heavy and light, intimate with the snow, they walked along in it as in a home. Occasionally they stopped and looked back at the two black men as at strange apparitions, even though the sight of Jews wasn't foreign to them. Out of breath, the brothers arrived home, dusk was already falling. They heard from a distance the singsong of the studying children. It came toward them, a motherly sound, a fatherly word, it carried their whole childhood toward them, it meant and contained all that they had seen, heard, smelled and felt since the hour of their birth: the singsong of the studying children. It contained the smell of hot and flavorful meals, the black and white shimmer that emanated from their father's beard and face, the echo of their mother's sighs and of Menuchim's whimpering tones, Mendel Singer's whispered prayers in the evening, millions of unnamable regular and special events. Both brothers reacted with the same stirrings to the melody that wafted through the snow toward them as they neared their father's house. Their hearts beat in the same rhythm. The door flew open before them, through the window their mother Deborah had long seen them coming.

"We've been taken!" said Jonas without a greeting.

All of a sudden a terrible silence fell over the room in which the children's voices had been sounding only a moment before, a silence without bounds, much vaster than the space it had captured, and yet born from the little word "taken" that Jonas had just spoken. In the middle of a word they had memorized the children broke off their studying. Mendel, who had been pacing up and down the room, stopped, looked into the air, raised his arms and lowered them again. The mother Deborah sat down on one of the two stools that always stood near the stove as if they had long been waiting for the opportunity to receive a grieving mother. Miriam, the daughter, groped her way backwards into the corner, her heart pounded loudly, she thought everyone could hear it. The children sat nailed to their seats. Their legs in colorfully striped wool socks, which had swung incessantly during the studying, hung lifelessly under the table. Outside it was snowing incessantly, and the soft white of the flakes streamed a pale shimmer through the window into the room and onto the faces of the silent people. A few times they heard the wood cinders crackle in the stove and a soft rattle of the doorposts when the wind shook them. The sticks still over their shoulders, the white bundles still on the sticks, the brothers stood at the door, messengers of misfortune and its children. Suddenly Deborah cried: "Mendel, go and run, ask people for advice!"

Mendel Singer grasped at his beard. The silence was banished, the children's legs began to swing gently, the brothers put down their bundles and their sticks and approached the table.

"What foolishness are you talking?" said Mendel Singer. "Where should I go? And whom should I ask for advice? Who will help a poor teacher, and how should anyone help me? What help do you expect from people, when God has punished us?"

Deborah didn't answer. For a while, she remained sitting completely still on the stool. Then she stood up, kicked it with her foot as if it were a dog, so that it tottered away with a clatter, grabbed her brown shawl, which had been lying like a hill of wool on the floor, wrapped her head and neck, tied the fringes at the back of her neck into a strong knot with a furious motion as if she wanted to strangle herself, turned red in the face, stood there hissing as if filled with boiling water, and suddenly spat, firing white saliva like a poison bullet before Mendel Singer's feet. And as if with that alone she had not sufficiently demonstrated her contempt, she sent a cry after the saliva, which sounded like a *phooey!* but could not be clearly understood. Before the dumbfounded onlookers could recover, she opened the door. An evil gust of wind poured white flakes into the room, blew into Mendel Singer's face, grasped the children by their hanging legs. Then the door slammed shut. Deborah was gone.

She ran aimlessly through the streets, always in the middle, a dark brown colossus, she rushed through the white snow until she sank in it. She got tangled in her clothes, fell, stood up with astonishing nimbleness, ran on, she still didn't know where, but she felt as if her feet were running by themselves toward a destination that her head did not yet know. Twilight fell faster than the flakes, the first yellow lights glimmered, the few people who came out of the houses to close the window shutters turned their heads to Deborah and looked after her for a long time, even though they were freezing. Deborah ran toward the cemetery. When she reached the small wooden gate, she fell down again. She pulled herself up, the gate refused to give way, snow had jammed it. Deborah threw her shoulders against it. Now she was inside. The wind howled over the graves. Today the dead seemed deader than usual. Out of twilight night grew swiftly, black, black and glowing with snow. In front of one of the first gravestones in the first row, Deborah sank down. With clammy fists, she freed it from the snow, as if she wanted to assure herself that her voice would reach the dead more easily if the muffling layer between her prayer and the ear of the blessed were cleared away. And then a cry burst from Deborah, which sounded as if it were coming from a horn with a human heart in it. This cry was heard in the whole little town, but was immediately forgotten. For the silence that followed in its wake was no longer heard. Deborah gasped out only a soft whimper at short intervals, a soft, motherly whimper, which the night swallowed, the snow buried, and only the dead heard.

IV

Not far from Mendel Singer's Kluczýsk relatives lived Kapturak, a man without age, without family, without friends, nimble and very busy, and intimate with the authorities. Deborah sought his help. Of the seventy rubles that Kapturak demanded before he would meet with his clients, she possessed only about twenty-five, secretly saved during the long years of tribulation, kept in a durable leather pouch under a floorboard known to her alone. Every Friday she lifted it up gently when she scrubbed the floor. To her motherly hope the difference of forty-five rubles seemed smaller than the sum she already possessed. For she added to it the years in which the money had accumulated, the privations to which each half a ruble owed its lastingness, and the many silent and hot pleasures of counting it.

Mendel Singer tried in vain to describe to her Kapturak's inaccessibility, his hard heart and his hungry pouch.

"What do you want, Deborah," said Mendel Singer, "the poor are powerless. God doesn't cast them golden stones from heaven, they don't win the lottery, and they must bear their lot in humble devotion. To the one He gives and from the other He takes away. I don't know why He is punishing us, first with the sick Menuchim and now with the healthy children. Ah, the poor man has it bad, when he has sinned and when he is ill, he has it bad. One should bear one's fate! Let the sons report for duty, they won't go to ruin! Against the will of heaven there is no power. 'From Him come the thunder and lightning, he arches over the whole earth, no one can escape Him' – so it is written."

But Deborah replied, her hand on her hip above the bunch of rusty keys: "Man must seek to help himself, and God will help him. So it is written, Mendel! You always know the wrong sentences by heart. Many thousands of sentences were written, but you remember all the superfluous ones! You've become so foolish because you teach children! You give them the little intellect you have, and they leave all their stupidity with you. You're a teacher, Mendel, a teacher!"

Mendel Singer wasn't vain about his intellect and his profession. But Deborah's words rankled him, her reproaches slowly gnawed away his good nature, and in his heart the little white flames of indignation were already flickering. He turned away to avoid seeing his wife's face. He felt as if he had already known it for a long time, far longer than since their wedding, perhaps since childhood. For long years it had seemed to him the same as on the day of his marriage. He had not seen how the flesh crumbled away from the cheeks like beautifully lime-washed mortar from a wall, how the skin stretched around the nose to hang all the more loosely in flaps under the chin, how the lids wrinkled into webs over the eyes, and how the black of the eyes dulled into a cool and sober brown, cool, sensible and hopeless. One day, he didn't remember when it could have been (perhaps it had happened the morning when he himself had been asleep and only one of his eyes had surprised Deborah before the mirror), one day the realization had come over him. It was like a second, repeated marriage, this time with the ugliness, with the bitterness, with the advancing age of his wife. He felt her closer, almost merged with him, inseparable and eternal, but intolerable, agonizing and even a little abhorrent. From a woman with whom one unites only in the darkness, she had become, so to speak, an illness to which one is bound day and night, which belongs entirely to oneself, which one no longer needs to share with the world and of whose faithful enmity one perishes. Certainly, he was only a teacher! His father too had been a teacher, and his grandfather. He himself simply couldn't be anything else. Thus one attacked his existence when one deprecated his profession, one tried to efface him from the list of the world. Against this Mendel Singer defended himself.

Actually he was glad that Deborah was going away. Now, as she was making preparations for her departure, the house was already empty: Jonas and Shemariah roamed the streets, Miriam sat with the neighbors or went for walks. At home, around the midday hour, before the pupils returned, only Mendel and Menuchim remained. Mendel ate a barley soup he had cooked himself, and left on his earthen plate a considerable portion for Menuchim. He bolted the door so that the little one wouldn't crawl out, as was his way. Then the father went into the corner, lifted the child, set him on his knee and began to feed him.

He loved those quiet hours. He was glad to be alone with his son. Indeed, sometimes he wondered whether it wouldn't be better if they remained alone altogether, without mother, without siblings. After Menuchim had swallowed the barley soup spoonful by spoonful, his father set him on the table, sat still before him, and became absorbed with tender curiosity in the broad pale yellow face with its wrinkled forehead, creased eyelids and flabby double chin. He sought to divine what might be going on in that broad head, to see through the eyes as through windows into the brain, and by speaking, now softly, now loudly, to elicit some sign from the impassive boy. He called Menuchim's name ten times in a row, with slow lips he drew the sound in the air so that Menuchim could see it if he couldn't hear it. But Menuchim didn't stir. Then Mendel grabbed his spoon, struck it against a tea glass, and immediately Menuchim turned his head, and a tiny light flashed in his large gray bulging eyes. Mendel kept ringing, began to sing a little song and to beat time with the spoon on the glass, and Menuchim displayed a distinct restlessness, turned his large head with some effort and swung his legs. "Mama, Mama!" he cried meanwhile. Mendel stood up, fetched the black book of the Bible, held the first page open before Menuchim's face and intoned, in the melody in which he usually taught his pupils, the first sentence: "In the beginning God created the heaven and the earth." He waited a moment in the hope that Menuchim would repeat the words. But Menuchim didn't stir. Only in his eyes the listening light remained. Then Mendel put the book away, looked sadly at his son, and went on in the monotonous singsong:

"Hear me, Menuchim, I am alone! Your brothers have grown big and strange, they're joining the army. Your mother is a woman, what can I expect of her? You are my youngest son, my last and most recent hope I have planted in you. Why are you silent, Menuchim? You are my true son! Look here, Menuchim, and repeat the words: 'In the beginning God created the heaven and the earth . . .'"

Mendel waited another moment. Menuchim didn't move. Then Mendel rang again with the spoon on the glass. Menuchim turned around, and Mendel seized the moment of alertness as if with both hands, and sang again: "Hear me, Menuchim! I am old, you alone of all my children remain with me, Menuchim! Listen and say after me: 'In the beginning God created the heaven and the earth . . . '" But Menuchim didn't move.

Then, with a heavy sigh, Mendel put Menuchim back down on the floor. He unbolted the door and stepped outside to wait for his pupils. Menuchim crawled after him and remained crouching at the threshold. The tower clock struck seven strokes, four deep ones and three high ones. Then Menuchim cried: "Mama, Mama!" And when Mendel turned to him, he saw that the little one was stretching his head into the air as if he were breathing in the resounding song of the bells.

Why have I been so punished? thought Mendel. And he searched his brain for some sin and found no grave one.

The pupils arrived. He returned with them into the house, and as he paced up and down the room, admonished this one and that, struck this one on the fingers and gave that one a light nudge in the ribs, he thought incessantly: Where is the sin? Where is the sin?

Meanwhile, Deborah went to the driver Sameshkin and asked him whether he could take her with him to Kluczýsk in the immediate future for free.

"Yes," said the coachman Sameshkin, he sat on the bare stove bench without moving, his feet in pale brown bags wound with ropes, and he stank of home-brewed schnapps. Deborah smelled the brandy as if it were an enemy. It was the dangerous smell of the peasants, the harbinger of incomprehensible passions and the accompaniment of pogrom moods. "Yes," said Sameshkin, "if the roads were better!" "You have taken me with you once before in autumn when the roads were even worse." "I don't remember," said Sameshkin, "you're mistaken, it must have been a dry summer day." "By no means," replied Deborah, "it was autumn, and it was raining, and I went to the rabbi." "You see," said Sameshkin, and his two feet in the bags began to swing gently, for the stove bench was rather high and Sameshkin rather small in stature, "you see," he said, "that time when you went to the rabbi, it was before your high holy days, and so I took you with me. But today you're not going to the rabbi!" "I'm going on important business," said Deborah, "Jonas and Shemariah must never become soldiers!" "I too was a soldier," declared Sameshkin, "for seven years, two of them I spent in prison, because I had stolen. A trifle, incidentally!" He drove Deborah to despair. His stories only proved to her how foreign he was to her, to her and to her sons, who would neither steal nor serve time in prison. So she decided to bargain quickly: "How much shall I pay you?" "Nothing at all! – I'm not asking for money, and I don't want to drive! The white horse is old, the brown one has just lost two horseshoes. Incidentally, he eats oats all day when he's gone only two versts. I can't keep him anymore, I want to sell him. It's no life at all, being a driver!" "Jonas will take the brown one to the blacksmith himself," Deborah said insistently, "he'll pay for the horseshoes himself." "Maybe!" replied

Sameshkin. "If Jonas wants to do that himself, then he has to have a wheel mounted too." "That too," Deborah promised. "So we'll leave next week!"

Thus she traveled to Kluczýsk, to the unearthly Kapturak. She would much rather have gone to the rabbi, for certainly one word from his holy, thin mouth was worth more than Kapturak's patronage. But the rabbi didn't receive anyone between Easter and Pentecost, except in urgent matters of life and death. She met Kapturak in the tavern, where he was sitting and writing, surrounded by peasants and Jews, in the corner by the window. His open cap, with the lining turned upward, lay on the table beside the papers like an outstretched hand, and many silver coins already rested in the cap and attracted the eyes of all the onlookers. Kapturak checked them from time to time, though he knew that no one would dare steal from him even one kopeck. He wrote applications, love letters and postal orders for every illiterate – (he could also pull teeth and cut hair).

"I have an important matter to discuss with you," Deborah said over the heads of the onlookers. Kapturak pushed all the papers away from him with one stroke, the people scattered, he reached for the cap, poured the money into his empty hand and tied it into a handkerchief. Then he invited Deborah to sit down.

She looked into his hard little eyes as into rigid light-colored buttons made of horn. "My sons have been conscripted!" she said. "You are a poor woman," said Kapturak with a remote singing voice, as if he were reading from the cards. "You have not been able to save any money, and no one can help you." "But I have saved." "How much?" "Twenty-four rubles and seventy kopecks. I've already spent one ruble of that to see you." "So that makes twenty-three rubles!" "Twenty-three rubles and seventy kopecks!" corrected Deborah. Kapturak raised his right hand, spread the middle and index fingers and asked: "And two sons?" "Two," whispered Deborah. "Just one already costs twenty-five!" "For me?" "For you too!" They bargained for half an hour. Then Kapturak declared himself content with twenty-three for one. At least one! thought Deborah.

But on the way back, as she sat on Sameshkin's cart and the wheels jolted her intestines and her poor head, the situation seemed to her still more miserable than before. How could she choose between her sons? Jonas or Shemariah? she asked herself tirelessly. Better one than both, said her intellect, lamented her heart.

When she arrived home and began to report Kapturak's judgment to her sons, Jonas, the older, interrupted her with the words: "I'll gladly join the army!" Deborah, the daughter Miriam, Shemariah and Mendel Singer waited as if they were made of wood. Finally, when Jonas said nothing more, Shemariah said: "You are a brother! You are a good brother!" "No," replied Jonas, "I want to join the army."

"Perhaps you will be released in half a year!" their father consoled.

"No," said Jonas, "I don't want to be released at all! I'm staying with the army!"

All murmured the bedtime prayer. Silently they undressed. Then Miriam went in her shirt on coquettish toes to the lamp and blew it out. They lay down to sleep.

The next morning Jonas had disappeared. They searched for him all morning. Not until late in the evening did Miriam catch sight of him. He was riding a white horse, wearing a brown jacket and a soldier's cap.

"Are you already a soldier?" Miriam called.

"Not yet," said Jonas, stopping the horse. "Say hello to Father and Mother. I'm staying with Sameshkin temporarily, until I report for duty. Tell them I couldn't stand it at home, but I'm very fond of you all!"

Then he whistled with a willow rod, pulled on the reins, and rode on.

From that point on, he was the driver Sameshkin's stable boy. He groomed the white horse and the brown one, slept with them in the stable, sucked in with open savoring nostrils their sharp scent of urine and sour sweat. He got the oats and the drinking buckets, mended the pens, trimmed the tails, hung new little bells on the yoke, filled the troughs, replaced the rotten hay in the two carts with dry hay, drank *samogonka* with Sameshkin, got drunk and impregnated the maids.

They wept for him at home as a lost one, but they did not forget
him. The summer began, hot and dry. The evenings sank late
and golden over the land. Outside Sameshkin's hut Jonas sat and
played accordion. He was very drunk and didn't recognize his
own father, who sometimes hesitantly crept by, a shadow that was
afraid of itself, a father who never ceased to be amazed that this
son had sprung from his own loins.

V

On the twentieth of August a messenger from Kapturak appeared
at Mendel Singer's home to fetch Shemariah. All had been expecting the messenger one of these days. But when he stood before
them in the flesh, they were surprised and frightened. He was
an ordinary man of ordinary stature and ordinary appearance,
with a blue soldier's cap on his head and a thin rolled cigarette
in his mouth. When they invited him to sit down and have some
tea, he declined. "I'd rather wait outside the house," he said in
a way that indicated he was accustomed to waiting outside. But
this very decision of the man's sent Mendel Singer's family into
still more intense excitement. Again and again they saw the blue-
capped man appear like a guard outside the window, and each
time their movements grew more furious. They packed Shemariah's things, a suit, phylacteries, provisions for the journey, a

bread knife. Miriam fetched the objects, bringing over more and more. Menuchim, whose head already reached the table, raised his chin curiously and stupidly, and incessantly babbled the one word he could: Mama. Mendel Singer stood by the window and drummed against the pane. Deborah wept soundlessly, her eyes sent one tear after another toward her contorted mouth. When Shemariah's bundle was ready, it appeared to all of them much too scanty, and they searched the room with helpless eyes so as to discover some other object. Until that moment they hadn't spoken. Now that the white bundle lay next to the stick on the table, Mendel Singer turned away from the window and toward the room and said to his son: .

"You will send us word immediately and as quickly as possible, don't forget!" Deborah sobbed aloud, spread her arms and embraced her son. For a long time they clasped each other. Then Shemariah pried himself loose, stepped up to his sister and kissed her with smacking lips on both cheeks. His father spread his hands over him in a blessing and hastily murmured something incomprehensible. Fearfully, Shemariah then approached the gawking Menuchim. For the first time it was necessary to embrace the sick child, and Shemariah felt as if it were not a brother he had to kiss, but a symbol that gives no answer. Everyone would have liked to say something more. But no one found a word. They knew that it was a farewell forever. In the best case, Shemariah would end up safe and sound abroad. In the worst case, he would be caught on the border, then executed or shot on the spot by the border guards. What are people supposed to say to each other when they're parting for life? Shemariah shouldered the bundle and pushed open the door with his foot. He didn't look back. The moment he stepped over the threshold he tried to forget the house and his whole family. Behind his back there sounded once more a loud cry from Deborah. The door closed. Sensing that his mother had fallen unconscious, Shemariah approached his escort.

"Just beyond the marketplace," said the man with the blue cap, "the horses are waiting for us." As they passed Sameshkin's hut, Shemariah stopped. He cast a glance into the little garden, then into the open empty stable. His brother Jonas wasn't there. He left a melancholy thought for his lost brother, who had voluntarily sacrificed himself, as Shemariah still believed. He's coarse, but noble and brave, he thought. Then he walked on with steady steps at the stranger's side.

Just beyond the marketplace they met the horses, as the man had said. It took them no less than three days to reach the border, for they avoided the railroad. Along the way it turned out that Shemariah's escort knew the country well. He revealed it without Shemariah's asking. He pointed to distant church steeples and named the villages to which they belonged. He named the farms and the estates and the landowners. He often branched off the wide road and found his way on narrow paths in a short time. It was as if he wanted to quickly make Shemariah familiar with his homeland, before the young man departed to seek a new one. He sowed homesickness for life in Shemariah's heart.

An hour before midnight they reached the border tavern. It was a quiet night. The tavern stood in it as the only house, a house in the stillness of the night, silent, dark, with sealed windows behind which no life could be suspected. A million crickets chirped around it incessantly, the whispering choir of the night. Otherwise no voice disturbed them. Flat was the land, the starry horizon drew a perfect deep blue circle around it, broken only in the northeast by a bright streak, like a blue ring with a setting of silver. They smelled the distant dampness of the swamps that spread out in the west and the slow wind that carried it over. "A beautiful true summer night!" said Kapturak's messenger. And for the first time since they were together, he deigned to speak of his business: "On such quiet nights you can't always cross without difficulties. For our purposes rain is more useful." He cast a little fear into Shemariah. Because the tavern before which they stood was silent and closed, Shemariah hadn't thought about its significance until his escort's words reminded him of his plan. "Let's go in!" he said like someone who no longer wants to postpone danger. "You don't need to hurry, we'll have to wait long enough!"

Nonetheless, he went to the window and knocked softly on the wooden shutter. The door opened and released a wide stream of yellow light over the nocturnal earth. They entered. Behind the counter, directly in the beam of a hanging lamp, the innkeeper stood and nodded at them, on the floor a few men were crouching and playing dice. At a table sat Kapturak with a man in a sergeant's uniform. No one looked up. The rattle of the dice and the tick of the wall clock could be heard. Shemariah sat down. His escort ordered drinks. Shemariah drank schnapps, he grew hot, but calm. He felt secure as never before; he knew that he was experiencing one of the rare hours in which a man has no less a part in shaping his destiny than the great power that bestows it on him.

Shortly after the clock had struck midnight, a shot rang out, hard and sharp, with a slowly dwindling echo. Kapturak and the sergeant rose. It was the arranged sign with which the guard indicated that the border officer's nightly patrol was over. The sergeant disappeared. Kapturak urged the people to set off. All rose sluggishly, shouldered bundles and suitcases, the door opened, they trickled out singly into the night and started on the way to the border. They tried to sing, someone forbade them, it was Kapturak's voice. They didn't know if it came from the front rows, from the middle, from the back. Thus they walked silently through the thick chirping of the crickets and the deep blue of the night. After half an hour Kapturak's voice commanded them: "Lie down!" They dropped onto the dewy ground, lay motionlessly, pressed their pounding hearts against the wet earth, their hearts' farewell to their homeland. Then they were ordered to stand up. They came to a shallow wide ditch, a light flashed to their left, it was the light of the guard hut. They crossed the ditch. Dutifully, but without aiming, the guard fired his rifle behind them.

"We're out!" cried a voice.

At that moment the sky brightened in the east. The men looked back to their homeland, over which the night still seemed to lie, and turned again toward the day and the foreign.

One began to sing, all joined in, singing they began to march. Only Shemariah did not sing along. He thought about his immediate future (he possessed two rubles); about the morning at home. In two hours at home his father would rise, murmur a prayer, clear his throat, gargle, go to the bowl and splash water. His mother would blow into the samovar. Menuchim would babble something into the morning, Miriam would comb white down feathers from her black hair. All this Shemariah saw more clearly than he had ever seen it when he was still at home and himself a part of the domestic morning. He scarcely heard the singing of the others, only his feet took up the rhythm and marched along.

An hour later he glimpsed the first foreign town, the blue smoke from the first diligent chimneys, a man with a yellow armband who received the arrivals. A tower clock struck six.

The Singers' wall clock also struck six. Mendel rose, gargled, cleared his throat, murmured a prayer, Deborah already stood at the stove and blew into the samovar, Menuchim babbled from his corner something incomprehensible, Miriam combed her hair in front of the murky mirror. Then Deborah slurped the hot tea, still standing at the stove. "Where is Shemariah now?" she said suddenly. All had been thinking of him.

"God will help him!" said Mendel Singer. And thus dawned the day.

And thus dawned the days that followed, empty days, miserable days. A house without children, thought Deborah. I bore them all, I suckled them all, a wind has blown them away. She looked around for Miriam, she rarely found her daughter at home. Menuchim alone remained with his mother. He always stretched out his arms when she passed his corner. And when she kissed him, he sought her breast like an infant. Reproachfully she thought of the blessing that was so slow in its fulfillment, and she doubted whether she would live to see Menuchim's health.

The house was silent when the singsong of the studying boys ceased. It was silent and dark. It was winter again. They saved petroleum. They lay down early to sleep. They sank thankfully into the kind night. From time to time Jonas sent a greeting. He served in Pskov, enjoyed his usual good health and had no difficulties with his superiors.

Thus the years passed.

VI

On a late summer afternoon a stranger entered the house of Mendel Singer. Door and window stood open. The flies clung still, black and sated to the hot sunlit walls, and the singsong of the pupils streamed from the open house into the white street. Suddenly they noticed the strange man in the doorframe and fell silent.

Deborah rose from her stool. From the other side of the street Miriam hurried over, holding the wobbling Menuchim firmly by the hand. Mendel Singer stood before the stranger and scrutinized him. He was an extraordinary man. He wore a mighty black high-crowned hat, wide light-colored flapping pants, sturdy yellow boots, and like a flag a bright red tie fluttered over his deep green shirt. Without moving, he said something, apparently a greeting, in an incomprehensible language. It sounded as if he were speaking with a cherry in his mouth. Green stems were sticking out of his coat pockets, anyhow. His smooth, very long upper lip rose slowly like a curtain and revealed a strong, yellow set of teeth reminiscent of horses. The children laughed, and even Mendel Singer smiled. The stranger pulled out a letter folded lengthwise and read the address and name of the Singers in his peculiar fashion, so that everyone laughed again. "America!" the man then said, and handed Mendel Singer the letter. A happy suspicion arose in Mendel and lit up his face. "Shemariah," he said. With a motion of his hand he sent off his pupils as one waves away flies. They ran out. The stranger sat down. Deborah set tea, sweets and soda on the table. Mendel opened the letter. Deborah and Miriam sat down too. And Singer began to read aloud the following:

Dear Father, dear Mother, precious Miriam and good Menuchim!
I don't address Jonas, because he is in the military. I also ask you not to send him this letter directly, because he might end up in adverse circumstances if he corresponds with a brother who is a

deserter. That's also why I have waited so long and not written to you by mail until I finally had the opportunity to send you this letter with my good friend Mac. He knows all of you from my stories, but he won't be able to speak a word with you, because not only is he an American, but his parents were born in America too, and he's not a Jew either. But he's better than ten Jews.

And so I'll tell you everything, from the beginning until today: At first, when I crossed the border, I had nothing to eat, only two rubles in my pocket, but I thought, God will help. From a Trieste shipping company a man with an official cap came to the border to pick us up. We were twelve men, the other eleven all had money, they bought false papers and ship tickets, and the agent of the shipping company brought them to the train. I went along. I thought, it can't do any harm. I'll go along, in any case I'll see how it is when you journey to America. So I stay behind alone with the agent, and he's surprised that I'm not going too. 'I don't have any kopecks,' I say to the agent. He asks whether I read and write. 'A little bit,' I say, 'but maybe it's enough.' Well, to be brief, the man had a job for me: every day, when the deserters arrive, go to the border, pick them up and buy them everything and persuade them that in America milk and honey flow. Well: I begin to work and give fifty percent of my earnings to the agent, because I'm only a sub-agent. He wears a cap with a gold-embroidered firm, I have only an armband. After two months I tell him I need sixty percent, or else I'll quit the job. He gives sixty. To make a long story short, I meet a pretty girl at my lodging, her name is Vega, and now she's your daughter-in-law. Her

father gave me some money to start a business, but I can never for-
get how the eleven went to America, and how I alone stayed behind.
So I take leave of Vega, I know all about ships, it's my trade after
all – and so I go to America. And here I am, two months ago Vega
came here, we got married and are very happy. Mac has the pictures
in his pocket. At first I sewed buttons on pants, then I ironed pants,
then I sewed linings in sleeves, and I almost would have become a
tailor, like all Jews in America. But then I met Mac on an excursion
to Long Island, right at Fort Lafayette. When you're here, I'll show
you the place. From then on I began to work with him, all sorts of
businesses. Until we took up insurance. I insure the Jews and he
the Irish, I've even insured a few Christians. Mac will give you ten
dollars from me, buy yourselves something with it, for the journey.
Because soon I will send you ship tickets, with God's help.

I embrace and kiss you all. Your son, Shemariah
(here my name is Sam)

After Mendel Singer had finished the letter, there was a ringing
silence in the room, which seemed to mingle with the stillness of
the late summer day and out of which all the members of the family
thought they heard the voice of the emigrated son. Yes, Shemariah
himself spoke, over there, worlds away in America, where at this
hour it was perhaps night or morning. For a short while, all forgot
Mac's presence. It was as if he had become invisible behind the distant Shemariah, like a mailman who delivers a letter, goes on and
disappears. He himself, the American, had to remind them of his

[61]

presence. He rose and reached into his pants pocket like a magician about to perform a trick. He pulled out a wallet, took out of it ten dollars and photographs, one of Shemariah with his wife Vega on a bench surrounded by greenery and another of him alone in a swimsuit on a beach, one body and one face among a dozen strange bodies and faces, no longer a Shemariah but a Sam. The stranger handed the ten-dollar bill and the pictures to Deborah, after he had briefly scrutinized them all, as if to check the trustworthiness of each one. She crumpled the bill in one hand, with the other she laid the pictures on the table next to the letter. All this lasted a few minutes, in which they remained silent. Finally Mendel Singer placed his index finger on the photograph and said: "That is Shemariah!" "Shemariah!" repeated the others, and even Menuchim, who now already reached above the table, uttered a high whinny and cast one of his shy glances with peering cautiousness at the pictures.

All of a sudden Mendel Singer felt as if the stranger were no longer a stranger, and as if he understood the man's peculiar language. "Tell me something!" he said to Mac. And the American, as if he had understood Mendel's words, began to move his large mouth and relate incomprehensible things with cheerful enthusiasm, and it was as if he were chewing up many a tasty dish with a healthy appetite. He told the Singers that he had come to Russia because of some business with hops – he was planning to build breweries in Chicago. But the Singers didn't understand him. Now that he was here, he definitely didn't want to miss visiting the Caucasus and especially climbing Mount Ararat, which he had read all about in the Bible. As the audience listened to Mac's story with strained hearkening gestures so as to catch out of the whole ranting jumble perhaps one tiny, comprehensible syllable, their hearts trembled at the word "Ararat," which seemed to them strangely familiar but also dismayingly altered, and which rolled out of Mac with a dangerous and terrible rumble. Mendel Singer alone smiled incessantly. He found it pleasant to hear the language that had now become that of his son Shemariah too, and as Mac talked, Mendel tried to imagine how his son looked when he spoke the same words. And soon he felt as if the voice of his own son were speaking from the cheerfully chomping mouth of the stranger. The American finished his talk, went around the table and squeezed everyone's hand heartily and firmly. Menuchim he swept swiftly into the air, observed the sloping head, the thin neck, the blue lifeless hands and the curved legs, and set him on the floor with a tender and pensive contempt, as if he wanted thus to express that strange creatures ought to crouch on the ground and not stand at tables. Then he walked, broad, tall and swaying a little, his hands in his pants pockets, out the open door, and the whole family jostled after him. All shaded their eyes with their hands as they looked into the sunny street, in the middle of which Mac strode away and at the end of which he stopped once more to give a brief wave back.

For a long time they stayed outside, even after Mac had disappeared. They held their hands over their eyes and looked into the dusty radiance of the empty street. Finally Deborah said: "Now he's gone!" And as if the stranger had only then disappeared, they all turned around and stood, each with an arm around the other's shoulder, in front of the photographs on the table. "How much are ten dollars?" Miriam asked, and began to calculate. "It doesn't matter," said Deborah, "how much ten dollars are, we're certainly not going to buy ourselves anything with it."

"Why not?" replied Miriam, "shall we travel in our rags?"

"Who is traveling and where?" cried the mother.

"To America," Miriam said with a smile, "Sam himself wrote it."

For the first time a member of the family had called Shemariah "Sam," and it was as if Miriam had intentionally spoken her brother's American name to lend emphasis to his demand that the family should travel to America.

"Sam!" cried Mendel Singer, "who is Sam?"

"Yes," repeated Deborah, "who is Sam?"

"Sam!" said Miriam, still smiling, "is my brother in America and your son!"

The parents were silent.

Menuchim's voice suddenly rang out shrilly from the corner into which he had crawled.

"Menuchim can't go!" Deborah said softly, as if she feared that the sick child could understand her.

"Menuchim can't go!" repeated, just as softly, Mendel Singer.

The sun seemed to sink rapidly. On the wall of the house across the street, at which they all stared through the open window, the black shadow rose visibly higher, as the sea climbs up its shoreline bluffs with the approach of the flood. A faint wind stirred, and the window creaked in its hinges.

"Close the door, there's a draft!" said Deborah.

Miriam went to the door. Before she touched the latch, she stood still for a moment and stuck her head out the doorframe in the direction in which Mac had disappeared. Then Miriam closed the door with a hard slam and said: "That's the wind!"

Mendel stood at the window. He watched as the shadow of evening crept up the wall. He raised his head and contemplated the gold-gleaming rooftop of the house across the street. He stood for a long time thus, the room, his wife, his daughter Miriam and the sick Menuchim at his back. He felt them all and sensed each of their movements. He knew that Deborah laid her head on the table to weep, that Miriam turned her face toward the stove and that her shoulders now and then jerked, even though she wasn't weeping at all. He knew that his wife was only waiting for the moment when he would reach for his prayer book to go to the temple and say the evening prayer, and Miriam would take the yellow shawl to hurry over to the neighbors. Then Deborah would bury the ten-dollar bill, which she still held in her hand, under the floorboard. He knew the floorboard, Mendel Singer. Whenever he stepped on it, it creakingly betrayed to him the secret it covered and reminded him of the growling of the dogs Sameshkin kept tethered outside his stable. He knew the board,

Mendel Singer. And so he wouldn't have to think of Sameshkin's black dogs, which were unearthly to him, living figures of sin, he avoided stepping on the board when he wasn't being forgetful and wandering through the room in the enthusiasm of teaching. As he saw the golden streak of the sun grow ever narrower and glide from the top ridge of the house onto the roof and from there onto the white chimney, he believed he felt distinctly for the first time in his life the soundless and wily creeping of the days, the deceptive treachery of the eternal alternation of day and night and summer and winter, and the stream of life, steady, despite all anticipated and unexpected terrors. They grew only on the changeful banks, Mendel Singer drifted past them. A man came from America, laughed, brought a letter, dollars and pictures of Shemariah and disappeared again into the veiled regions of the distance. The sons disappeared: Jonas served the Tsar in Pskov and was no longer Jonas. Shemariah bathed on the shores of the ocean and was no longer called Shemariah. Miriam gazed after the American and wanted to go to America too. Only Menuchim remained what he had been since the day of his birth: a cripple. And Mendel Singer himself remained what he had always been: a teacher.

The narrow street darkened completely and came to life at the same time. The fat wife of the glazier Chaim and the ninety-year-old grandmother of the long dead locksmith Yossel Kopp brought chairs out of their houses to sit down outside the doors and enjoy the fresh evening hour. The Jews rushed, black and hurried and with hastily murmured greetings, to the temple. Then Mendel

Singer turned around, he wanted to set off too. He passed Deborah, whose head still lay on the hard table. Her face, which Mendel had not been able to bear for years, was now buried, as if embedded in the hard wood, and the darkness that began to fill the room also covered Mendel's hardness and shyness. His hand glided over his wife's broad back, this flesh had once been familiar to him, now it was strange to him. She rose and said: "You go to pray!" And because she was thinking of something else, she modified the sentence with a distant voice and repeated: "To pray you go!"

At the same time as her father, Miriam left the house in her yellow shawl and proceeded to the neighbors.

It was the first week in the month of Av. The Jews gathered after the evening prayer to greet the new moon, and because the night was pleasant and refreshing after the hot day, they followed more willingly than usual their devout hearts and God's commandment to greet the rebirth of the moon in an open place over which the sky arched more widely and vastly than over the narrow streets of the little town. And they hastened, silent and black, in disorderly little groups, behind the houses, saw in the distance the forest, which was black and silent like them, but eternal in its rooted persistence, saw the veils of night over the wide fields and finally stopped. They looked to the sky and sought the curved silver of the new heavenly body that today was born once again as on the day of its creation. They formed a tight group, opened their prayer books, white shimmered the pages, black stared the angular letters before their eyes in the night's bluish clearness, and they began to murmur the greeting to the moon and to rock their upper bodies back and forth so that they looked as if shaken by an invisible storm. Ever faster they rocked, ever louder they prayed, with warlike courage they cast to the distant heaven their foreign words. Alien to them was the earth on which they stood, hostile the forest, which stared back at them, spiteful the yapping of the dogs, whose mistrustful ears they had awakened, and familiar only the moon, which was born today in this world as in the land of the fathers, and the Lord, who was everywhere watching over, at home and in exile.

With a loud "Amen" they concluded the blessing, shook hands with each other and wished each other a happy month, prosperity for the businesses and health for the sick. They parted, walked home singly, disappeared in the narrow passages behind the little doors of their slanting huts. Only one Jew stayed behind, Mendel Singer.

His companions might have left only a few minutes earlier, but he felt as if he had already been standing there for an hour. He breathed the undisturbed peace in the open, took a few steps, felt weary, had an urge to lie down on the ground and was afraid of the unknown earth and the dangerous worms it most likely harbored. His lost son Jonas came to his mind. Jonas now slept in barracks, on the hay, in a stable, perhaps next to horses. His son Shemariah lived on the other side of the water: Who was farther, Jonas or Shemariah? Deborah had already buried the dollars at home, and Miriam was now telling the neighbors the story of the American's visit.

The young crescent moon was already shedding a strong silver glow, faithfully accompanied by the brightest star of the sky it glided through the night. Occasionally the dogs howled and frightened Mendel. They rent the peace of the earth and increased Mendel Singer's unease. Though he was scarcely five minutes away from the houses of the little town, he felt infinitely far from the inhabited world of the Jews, inexpressibly alone, threatened by dangers and yet incapable of going back. He turned northward: there the forest breathed darkly. On the right the swamps, with scattered silver willows, stretched for many versts. On the left the fields lay under opalescent veils. Sometimes Mendel thought he heard a human sound from an indeterminable direction. He heard familiar people talking, and he felt as if he understood them. Then he remembered that he had heard those voices long ago. He realized that he was now only hearing them again, merely their echo, which had been waiting so long in his memory. All of a sudden there was a rustling to the left in the grain, even though no wind had stirred. The rustling came closer and closer, now Mendel could also see the head-high grain moving, a person must be creeping through, if not a gigantic animal, a monster. To run away would probably have been right, but Mendel waited and prepared for death. A peasant or a soldier would now emerge from the grain, accuse Mendel of theft and beat him to death on the spot – with a stone perhaps. It could also be a tramp, a murderer, a criminal, who doesn't want to be heard and seen. "Holy God!" whispered Mendel. Then he heard voices. It was two people walking through the grain, and that it wasn't one calmed the Jew, even though he told himself at the same time that it could be two murderers. No, it wasn't murderers, it was lovers. A girl's voice spoke, a man laughed. Even lovers could be dangerous, there was many an example of a man flying into a rage when he caught a witness to his love. Soon the two would emerge from the field. Mendel Singer overcame his fearful disgust for the worms of the earth and lay down quietly, his eyes directed at the grain. Then the grain parted, the man emerged first, a man in uniform, a soldier with a dark blue cap, booted and spurred, the metal flashed and rang softly. Behind him a yellow shawl gleamed, a yellow shawl, a yellow shawl. A voice sounded, the voice of the girl. The soldier turned around, put his arm around her shoulders, now the shawl opened, the soldier went behind the girl, he held his hands on her breast, the girl embedded herself in the soldier.

Mendel closed his eyes and let the misfortune pass by in the darkness. Had he not been afraid of revealing himself, he would have liked to plug his ears too, so that he wouldn't have to hear. But as it was he had to hear: terrible words, the silver rattle of the spurs, soft mad giggling and the man's deep laugh. Longingly he now awaited the yapping of the dogs. If only they would howl loudly, they should howl very loudly! Murderers should emerge from the grain to beat him to death. The voices receded. It was silent. All was gone. Nothing had been. Mendel Singer hastily stood up, looked all around, lifted with both hands the skirts of his long coat and ran toward the little town. The window shutters were closed, but some women were still sitting outside their doors, chatting and rasping. He slowed his run to avoid attracting attention, he merely took great hurried strides, his coattails still in his hands. He stood before his house. He knocked on the window. Deborah opened it. "Where's Miriam?" asked Mendel. "She's still taking a walk," said Deborah, "she can't be stopped! Day and night she goes walking. She's in the house for barely half an hour. God has punished me with these children, has anyone ever in the world – " "Be quiet," Mendel interrupted her, "when Miriam comes home, tell her: I was asking for her. I'm not coming home today, but only tomorrow morning. Today is the anniversary of the death of my grandfather Zallel, I'm going to pray." And he departed without waiting for his wife's reply.

It could scarcely have been three hours since he'd left the temple. Now that he entered it again, he felt as if he were returning there after many weeks, and he stroked with a tender hand the lid of his old prayer desk and celebrated a reunion with it. He opened it and reached for his old, black and heavy book, which was at home in his hands and which he would have recognized without hesitation among a thousand similar books. So familiar to him was the leather smoothness of the binding with the raised round islets of stearin, the encrusted remains of countless candles burned long ago, and the lower corners of the pages, porous, yellowish, greasy, curled three times over through decades of being turned with moistened fingers. Any prayer he needed at the moment he could open to in no time. It was engraved in his memory with the tiniest features of the physiognomy it bore in this prayer book, the number of its lines, the nature and size of the print and the exact shading of the pages.

It was twilight in the temple, the yellowish light of the candles on the eastern wall next to the cabinet of the Torah scrolls did not dispel the darkness, but rather seemed to bury itself in it. He saw the sky and a few stars through the windows and recognized all the objects in the room, the desks, the table, the benches, the scraps of paper on the floor, the candelabra on the wall, a few golden-fringed little covers. Mendel Singer lit two candles, stuck them to the bare wood of the desk, closed his eyes and began to pray. With closed eyes he knew where a page ended, mechanically he turned to the next. Gradually his upper body slipped into the old customary regular swaying, his whole body prayed with him, his feet scraped the floorboards, his hands closed into fists and pounded like hammers on the desk, on his chest, on the book and in the air. On the stove bench slept a homeless Jew. His breaths accompanied and supported Mendel Singer's monotonous song, which was like a hot song in the yellow desert, lost and intimate with death. His own voice and the breath of the sleeper benumbed

Mendel, drove every thought out of his heart, he was nothing more than one praying, the words went through him on the way to heaven, a hollow vessel he was, a funnel. Thus he prayed into the morning.

The day breathed on the windows. The lights became scanty and dull, behind the low huts one already saw the sun rising, it filled the two eastern windows of the temple with red flames. Mendel snuffed out the candles, put away the book, opened his eyes and turned to go. He stepped outside. It smelled of summer, drying swamps and awakened green. The window shutters were still closed. People were asleep.

Mendel knocked three times with his hand on his door. He was strong and fresh, as if he had slept dreamlessly and long. He knew exactly what was to be done. Deborah opened. "Make me some tea," said Mendel, "then I want to tell you something. Is Miriam home?" "Of course," replied Deborah, "where else would she be? Do you think she's already in America?"

The samovar hummed, Deborah breathed into a drinking glass and polished it. Then Mendel and Deborah drank steadily with pursed slurping lips. Suddenly Mendel put down the glass and said: "We will go to America. Menuchim must stay behind. We must take Miriam with us. A misfortune hovers over us if we stay." He remained silent for a while and then said softly:

"She's going with a Cossack."

The glass fell clanging from Deborah's hands. Miriam awoke

in the corner, and Menuchim stirred in his dull sleep. Then it remained silent. A million larks were trilling above the house, below the sky.

With a bright flash the sun struck the window, reached the shiny tin samovar and lit it into a curved mirror.

Thus the day began.

VII

To Dubno one travels with Sameshkin's cart; to Moscow one travels by railroad; to America one travels not only on a ship, but also with documents. And to get those one must go to Dubno.

Thus Deborah pays a visit to Sameshkin. Sameshkin is no longer sitting on the stove bench, he's not home at all, it's Thursday and the pig market, Sameshkin won't return home for an hour.

Deborah walks up and down, up and down outside Sameshkin's hut, she thinks only of America.

A dollar is more than two rubles, a ruble is a hundred kopecks, two rubles are two hundred kopecks, how many kopecks, for God's sake, are in a dollar? How many more dollars will Shemariah send? America is a blessed country.

Miriam is going with a Cossack, in Russia she can do that, in America there are no Cossacks. Russia is a sad country, America is a free country, a joyful country. Mendel will no longer be a teacher, he'll be the father of a rich son.

It doesn't take one hour, it doesn't take two hours, only after three hours does Deborah hear Sameshkin's nailed boots.

It's evening, but still hot. The slanting sun has already turned yellow, but it doesn't want to disappear, it's setting very slowly today. Deborah is sweating from heat and excitement and a hundred unfamiliar thoughts.

Now that Sameshkin is approaching, she becomes even hotter. He's wearing a heavy bearskin cap, shaggy and in some places mangy, and a short fur coat over dirty linen pants, which are tucked into the heavy boots. And yet he's not sweating.

The moment Deborah sees him she already smells him too, because he stinks of brandy. She's going to have a tough time with him. It's no small matter to bring around even the sober Sameshkin. On Monday the pig market is in Dubno. It doesn't help that Sameshkin has already visited the pig market at home, he'll probably have no more reason to go to Dubno, and the journey will cost money.

Deborah steps directly into Sameshkin's path. He staggers, the heavy boots hold him upright. "Lucky that he's not barefoot!" thinks Deborah, not without contempt.

Sameshkin doesn't recognize the woman blocking his way. "Away with the women!" he cries, and makes a motion with his hand, half grabbing and half striking.

"It's me!" Deborah says bravely. "Monday we're going to Dubno!"

"God bless you!" Sameshkin cries amiably. He stands still and leans with his elbow on Deborah's shoulder. She's afraid to move, lest Sameshkin fall down.

Sameshkin weighs a good seventy kilos, his whole weight now rests on the elbow, and this elbow rests on Deborah's shoulder.

It's the first time a strange man has been so close to her. She's frightened, but at the same time she thinks that she's already old, she also thinks of Miriam's Cossack and how long it's been since Mendel has touched her.

"Yes, my sweet," says Sameshkin, "Monday we're going to Dubno, and on the way we'll sleep together."

"Phooey, you old man," says Deborah, "I'll tell your wife, maybe you're drunk?"

"Drunk he is not," replies Sameshkin, "he has only been drinking. What do you want in Dubno anyway, if you won't sleep with Sameshkin?"

"To get documents," says Deborah, "we're going to America."

"The journey costs fifty kopecks if you don't sleep with him and thirty if you do. He'll make you a little child, you'll have it in America, a memento of Sameshkin."

Deborah shivers in the midst of the heat.

Nonetheless, she says, but only after a minute: "I won't sleep with you and will pay thirty-five kopecks."

Sameshkin suddenly stands back, he's pulled away his elbow from Deborah's shoulder, it seems that he's become sober.

"Thirty-five kopecks!" he says with a firm voice.

"Monday morning at five."

"Monday morning at five."

Sameshkin turns at his farm, and Deborah walks slowly home. The sun has set. The wind is coming from the west, on the horizon violet clouds are piling up, tomorrow it will rain. Deborah thinks, tomorrow it will rain, and feels a rheumatic pain in her knee, she greets it, her old faithful enemy. A person grows old! she thinks. Women age faster than men, Sameshkin is just as old as she and still older. Miriam is young, she's going with a Cossack.

The word "Cossack," which she had said aloud, frightened Deborah. It was as if only the sound had made her aware of the dreadfulness of the situation. At home she saw her daughter Miriam and her husband Mendel. They sat at the table, father and daughter, and were stubbornly silent, so that Deborah knew as soon as she entered that it was already an old silence, a domestic, firmly settled silence.

"I've spoken with Sameshkin," Deborah began. "Monday morning at five I'm going to Dubno for the documents. He wants thirty-five kopecks." And because she had been seized by the devil of vanity, she added: "He takes only me so cheaply."

"You can't go alone anyway," said, weariness in his voice and dread in his heart, Mendel Singer. "I've spoken with many Jews who know all about it. They say I must appear before the *uriadnik* myself."

"You before the *uriadnik*?"

It was indeed not easy to imagine Mendel Singer in an office. Never in his life had he spoken with an *uriadnik*. Never had he been able to encounter a police officer without trembling. Uniformed men, horses and dogs he carefully avoided. Mendel was going to speak with an *uriadnik*?

"Don't concern yourself, Mendel," said Deborah, "with things that you can only ruin. I'll sort everything out on my own."

"All the Jews," Mendel objected, "have told me that I must appear personally."

"Then we'll go together on Monday!"

"And where will Menuchim be?"

"Miriam will stay with him!"

Mendel looked at his wife. He tried with his glance to meet her eyes, which she hid fearfully under her lids. Miriam, who was gazing from a corner at the table, could see her father's glance, her heart quickened. Monday she had a rendezvous. Monday she had a rendezvous. The whole hot period of late summer she had a rendezvous. Her love blossomed late, among the high grain, Miriam was afraid of the harvest. She already sometimes heard the peasants preparing, sharpening the sickles on the blue whetstones. Where would she go when the fields were bare? She had to go to America. A vague idea of the freedom of love in America, among the tall buildings, which concealed still better than the grain in the field, consoled her about the approach of the harvest. It was already coming. Miriam had no time to lose. She loved Stepan. He would stay behind. She loved all men, storms broke from them, their powerful hands nonetheless gently lit flames in the heart. The men were named Stepan, Ivan and Vsevolod. In America there were many more men. "I'm not staying home alone," said Miriam, "I'm afraid!"

"We should," Mendel blurted out, "put a Cossack in the house for her. To guard her."

Miriam turned red. She believed that her father saw her redness, even though she stood in the corner, in the shadow. Her redness must be shining through the darkness, Miriam's face was inflamed like a red lamp. She covered it with her hands and burst into tears.

"Go out!" said Deborah, "it's late, close the shutters!"

She felt her way out, carefully, her hands still before her eyes. Outside she stopped for a moment. All the stars of the sky stood there, near and alive, as if they had been waiting for Miriam outside the house. Their clear golden splendor contained the splendor of the great free world, they were tiny mirrors, in which the glow of America was reflected.

She went to the window, looked in, tried to discern from her parents' facial expressions what they might be saying. She discerned nothing. She removed the iron hooks from the wood of the open shutters and closed both wings like the doors of a cabinet. She thought of a coffin. She was burying her parents in the little house. She felt no melancholy. Mendel and Deborah Singer were buried. The world was wide and alive. Stepan, Ivan and Vsevolod were alive. America was alive, on the other side of the great water, with all its tall buildings and with millions of men.

When she entered the room again, her father, Mendel Singer, said:

"She can't even close the shutters, it takes her half an hour!"

He groaned, rose and went to the wall on which the small petroleum lamp hung, dark blue container, sooty chimney, bound by a rusty wire to a cracked round mirror, which had the task of enhancing the sparse light at no cost. The opening at the top of the chimney was higher than Mendel Singer's head. He tried in vain to blow out the lamp. He stood on tiptoe, he blew, but the wick only flared up more strongly.

Meanwhile Deborah lit a small yellowish wax candle and put it on the brick stove. Mendel Singer climbed with a croak onto an armchair and finally blew out the lamp. Miriam lay down in the corner next to Menuchim. Not until it was dark would she undress. She waited breathlessly, with closed eyelids, until her father had finished murmuring his bedtime prayer. Through a round knothole in the window shutter she saw the blue and golden shimmer of the night. She undressed and touched her breasts. They hurt her. Her skin had its own memory and remembered in every place the large, hard and hot hands of the men. Her smell had its own memory and retained the fragrance of men's sweat, brandy and Russian leather incessantly, with tormenting faithfulness. She heard her parents' snoring and Menuchim's rattling breath. Then Miriam rose, in her shirt, barefoot, with her heavy braids, which she brought forward and the ends of which reached her thighs, unbolted the door and stepped out into the strange night. She breathed deeply. It seemed to her that she breathed in the whole night, all the golden stars she swallowed with her breath, still more kept burning in the sky. Frogs croaked and crickets chirped, the northeast edge of the sky was lined by a broad silver streak in which the morning seemed already to be contained. Miriam thought of the grain field, her marriage bed. She walked around the house. The great white wall of the barracks shimmered from afar. It sent a few meager lights toward Miriam. In a large room slept Stepan, Ivan and Vsevolod and many other men.

Tomorrow was Friday. Everything had to be prepared for Saturday, the meatballs, the pike and the chicken broth. The baking already began at six in the morning. As the broad silver streak turned reddish, Miriam crept back into the room. She didn't fall asleep. Through the knothole in the window shutter she saw the first flames of the sun. Father and Mother were already stirring in their sleep. Morning was there. The Sabbath passed, Sunday Miriam spent in the grain field, with Stepan. In the end they went far out, into the next village, Miriam drank schnapps. All day they looked for her at home. Let them look for her! Her life was precious, the summer was short, soon the harvest was beginning. In the forest she slept with Stepan again. Tomorrow, Monday, her father was going to Dubno to get the papers.

At five in the morning, on Monday, Mendel Singer rose. He drank tea, prayed, then quickly took off the phylacteries and went to Sameshkin. "Good morning!" he called from a distance. Mendel Singer felt as if the official business had already begun here, before climbing into Sameshkin's cart, and as if he had to greet Sameshkin as he would an *uriadnik*.

"I'd rather go with your wife!" said Sameshkin. "She's still good-looking for her years and has a decent bosom."

"Let's go," said Mendel.

The horses whinnied and struck their hindquarters with their tails. "Hey! Whoa!" cried Sameshkin, and cracked the whip.

At eleven in the morning they arrived in Dubno. Mendel had to wait. He stepped, his cap in his hand, through the large portal. The porter carried a saber.

"Where do you want to go?" he asked.

"I want to go to America – where do I have to go?"

"What's your name?"

"Mendel Mechelovich Singer."

"Why do you want to go to America?"

"To earn money, I'm doing badly."

"You go to number eighty-four," said the porter. "Many are already waiting there."

They sat in a large, arched, ocher-washed corridor. Men in

blue uniforms stood guard outside the doors. Along the walls were brown benches – all the benches were occupied. But whenever a newcomer arrived, the blue men made a hand motion; and those who were already sitting moved together, and each newcomer took a seat. They smoked, spat, cracked squash seeds and snored. Here the day was no day. Through the milk glass of a very high, very distant skylight, a pale intimation of the day could be glimpsed. Clocks were ticking somewhere, but they went, so to speak, alongside time, which in these high corridors stood still. Sometimes a man in blue uniform called out a name. All the sleepers awoke. The one who had been called rose, staggered toward a door, adjusted his suit and stepped through one of the high double doors, which instead of a latch had a round white knob. Mendel considered how he would handle this knob so as to open the door. He stood up; from sitting for a long time wedged between the people, his limbs were hurting him. But no sooner had he risen than a blue man approached him. "Sidai!" cried the blue man, "sit down!" Mendel Singer no longer found a seat on his bench. He remained standing next to it, pressed himself against the wall and wished he could become as flat as the wall.

"Are you waiting for number eighty-four?" asked the blue man. "Yes," said Mendel. He was convinced that they now intended to throw him out for good. Deborah will have to come here again. Fifty kopecks and fifty kopecks make a ruble.

But the blue man had no intention of sending Mendel out of the building. For the blue man the most important thing was that all the people waiting kept their seats and that he could survey them all. If one stood up, he could throw a bomb.

"Anarchists disguise themselves sometimes," thought the doorkeeper. And he beckoned Mendel over to him, patted down the Jew, asked for his papers. And because everything was in order and Mendel no longer had a seat, the blue man said: "Listen! See the glass door? Open it. There is number eighty-four!"

"What do you want here?" shouted a broad-shouldered man behind the desk. The official sat directly under the picture of the Tsar. He consisted of a mustache, a bald head, epaulets and buttons. He was like a beautiful bust behind his broad inkwell of marble. "Who permitted you to enter here just like that? Why don't you announce yourself?" a voice roared from the bust.

Mendel Singer meanwhile bowed deeply. He had not been prepared for such a reception. He bowed and let the thunder glide away over his back, he wanted to become tiny, level with the ground, as if he had been surprised by a storm in an open field. The folds of his long coat parted, and the official saw a bit of Mendel Singer's threadbare pants and the scuffed leather of his boot shafts. This sight made the official milder. "Come closer!" he commanded, and Mendel moved closer, his head bent forward as if he wanted to push his way to the desk. Only when he saw that he was approaching the edge of the carpet did Mendel Singer lift his head a little. The official smiled. "Give me the papers!" he said.

Then it was quiet. One heard the clock ticking. Through the

blinds broke the golden light of a late afternoon. The papers rustled. Occasionally the official mused for a while, gazed into the air, and suddenly snatched a fly with his hand. He held the tiny animal in his gigantic fist, opened it carefully, pulled off a wing, then the other, and continued to watch a bit as the crippled insect crawled on the desk.

"The application?" he asked suddenly, "where's the application?"

"I can't write, your Excellency!" Mendel apologized.

"I know that, you fool, that you can't write! I wasn't asking for your school certificate, but for the application. And why do we have a clerk? Huh? On the ground floor? In number three? Huh? Why does the state employ a clerk? For you, you idiot, just because you can't write. So go to number three. Write the application. Say I sent you, so that you don't have to wait and are attended to at once. Then come to me. But tomorrow! And tomorrow afternoon, as far as I'm concerned, you can leave!" Once again Mendel bowed. He walked backwards, he dared not turn his back to the official, the path from the desk to the door seemed to him infinitely long. He believed he'd already been walking for an hour. Finally he felt the nearness of the door. He turned around quickly, grabbed the knob, turned it first left, then right, then he gave another bow. Finally he stood again in the corridor.

In number three sat an ordinary official without epaulets. It was a musty low room, many people surrounded the table, the clerk wrote and wrote, he pushed the quill impatiently each time into the bottom of the ink container. He wrote nimbly, but he was never finished. New people always came. Nonetheless, he still had time to notice Mendel.

"His Excellency, the gentleman from number eighty-four, sent me," said Mendel.

"Come here," said the clerk.

The people cleared the way for Mendel Singer.

"One ruble for the stamp!" said the clerk. Mendel fished a ruble out of his blue handkerchief. It was a hard, shiny ruble. The clerk didn't take the coin, he expected at least another fifty kopecks. Mendel understood nothing of the clerk's rather clear wishes.

Then the clerk became angry. "Are those papers?" he said. "They're scraps! They crumble in one's hand!" And he tore one of the documents, as if unintentionally, it ripped into two equal pieces, and the official reached for the gum arabic to stick it together. Mendel Singer trembled.

The gum arabic was too dry, the official spat into the little bottle, then he breathed on it. But it remained dry. He suddenly had an idea, one saw by looking at him that he suddenly had an idea. He opened a drawer, put Mendel Singer's papers into it, closed it again, tore from a pad a little green slip of paper, stamped it, gave it to Mendel, and said: "You know what? Tomorrow morning at nine o'clock, you come here! Then we'll be alone. Then we can talk calmly with each other. Your papers are here with me. You fetch them tomorrow. Show the slip of paper!"

Mendel left. Sameshkin was waiting outside, he was sitting next to the horses on the stones, the sun was setting, the evening was coming.

"We're not leaving until tomorrow," said Mendel, "at nine o'clock I have to come back."

He searched for a temple where he could spend the night. He bought a piece of bread, two onions, put everything in his pocket, stopped a Jew and asked him about the temple. "Let's go together," said the Jew.

On the way Mendel told his story.

"In our temple," said the Jew, "you can meet a man who will deal with the whole matter for you. He's already sent many families to America. Do you know Kapturak?"

"Kapturak? Of course! He sent my son away!"

"Old clients!" said Kapturak. In late summer he stayed in Dubno, he held his meetings in the temples. "That time your wife came to me. I still remember your son. He's doing well, eh? Kapturak has a lucky hand."

It turned out that Kapturak was willing to take over the matter. For the time being it cost ten rubles per head. Mendel couldn't pay an advance of ten rubles. Kapturak knew a way out. He got the address of young Singer. In four weeks he'll have a reply and money, if the son really intends to bring over his parents. "Give me the green slip of paper, the letter from America, and rely on me!" said Kapturak. And the onlookers nodded. "Go home today. In a few days I'll come by. Rely on Kapturak!"

A few onlookers repeated: "You can rely on Kapturak!"

"It's lucky," said Mendel, "that I met you here!" All offered him their hands and wished him a good journey. He returned to the marketplace where Sameshkin was waiting. Sameshkin was just about to lie down to sleep in his wagon.

"With a Jew only the devil can arrange something certain!" he said. "So we're leaving after all!"

They set off.

Sameshkin tied the reins around his wrist, he intended to sleep a little. He actually nodded off, the horses shied at the shadow of a scarecrow that some rascal had carried out of a field and put on the roadside. The animals broke into a gallop, the cart seemed to rise into the air, soon, Mendel thought, it would begin to flutter, it seemed to him as if his heart was galloping too, it wanted to leave his breast and leap into the distance.

Suddenly Sameshkin uttered a loud curse. The cart slid into a ditch, the horses' forelegs were still jutting into the road, Sameshkin was lying on Mendel Singer.

They climbed out again. The shaft was splintered, a wheel had come loose, another was missing two spokes. They had to spend the night here. Tomorrow they would see.

"So your journey to America begins," said Sameshkin. "Why do you people always roam around so much in the world! The devil sends you from one place to another. Our sort stays where he's born, and only when there's a war, we move to Japan!"

Mendel Singer was silent. He was sitting on the roadside next to Sameshkin. For the first time in his life Mendel sat on the naked earth, in the middle of the wild night, next to a peasant. He saw above him the sky and the stars and thought, they conceal God. All this the Lord created in seven days. And when a Jew wants to go to America, it takes years!

"Do you see how beautiful the country is?" asked Sameshkin. "Soon the harvest will come. It is a good year. If it is as good as I imagine, I'll buy another horse in autumn. Do you hear anything from your son Jonas? He knows something about horses. He's completely different from you. Has your wife ever deceived you?" "Everything is possible," replied Mendel. He felt suddenly very light, he could comprehend everything, the night freed him from prejudices. He even snuggled up to Sameshkin, as to a brother.

"Everything is possible," he repeated, "women are no good."

Suddenly Mendel began to sob. Mendel wept, in the middle of the strange night, next to Sameshkin.

The peasant pressed his fists against his eyes, because he felt that he too would weep.

Then he put his arm around Mendel's thin shoulders and said softly:

"Sleep, dear Jew, sleep well."

He stayed awake for a long time. Mendel Singer slept and snored. The frogs croaked until morning.

VIII

Two weeks later a small, two-wheeled wagon rolled in a great dust cloud in front of Mendel Singer's house and brought a guest: it was Kapturak.

He reported that the papers were ready. Should a reply come from America in four weeks from Shemariah, known as Sam, the departure of the Singer family would be assured. That was all Kapturak had wanted to say; and that an advance of twenty rubles would be more agreeable to him than having to deduct the money later from Shemariah's sum.

Deborah went into the storeroom made of rotten wooden boards, which stood in the courtyard, pulled her blouse over her head, took a knotted handkerchief from her bosom and counted eight hard rubles into her hand.

Then she pulled the blouse back on, went into the house and said to Kapturak: "This is all I could scrape up from the neighbors. You have to be content with it."

"For an old client one lets some things pass," said Kapturak, jumped onto his small feather-light yellow wagon, and disappeared immediately in a dust cloud.

"Kapturak was at Mendel Singer's house!" cried the people in the little town. "Mendel is going to America."

Indeed, Mendel Singer's journey to America had already begun. All the people gave him advice against seasickness. A few buyers came to view Mendel's little house. They were prepared to pay a thousand rubles for it, a sum for which Deborah would have given five years of her life.

But Mendel Singer said: "You do know, Deborah, that Menuchim must stay behind? With whom will he stay? Next month Billes is marrying his daughter to Fogl the musician. Until they have a child, the young people can keep Menuchim. For that we will give them the house and take no money."

"Is the matter already settled for you, that Menuchim is staying behind? There are still at least a few weeks until our departure, by then God will surely perform a miracle."

"If God wants to perform a miracle," replied Mendel, "He won't let it be known beforehand. One must hope. If we don't go to America, a misfortune will occur with Miriam. If we go to America, we leave Menuchim behind. Shall we send Miriam to America alone? Who knows what she will do, alone on the way and alone in America. Menuchim is so sick that only a miracle can help him. But if a miracle helps him, he can follow us. Because America is indeed very far; but it doesn't lie outside this world."

Deborah remained silent. She heard the words of the rabbi of Kluczýsk: "Do not leave him, stay with him, as if he were a healthy child!" She was not staying with him. Long years, day and night, hour after hour, she had waited for the promised miracle. The dead in the beyond didn't help, the rabbi didn't help, God refused to help. She had wept a sea of tears. Night had been in her heart, sorrow in every pleasure, ever since Menuchim's birth. All festivals were torments, and all holidays days of mourning. There was no more spring and no summer. All seasons were winter. The sun rose, but it did not warm. Hope alone refused to die. "He will remain a cripple," said all the neighbors. For no misfortune had befallen them, and he who has no misfortune does not believe in miracles.

Nor does he who has misfortune believe in miracles. Miracles happened very long ago, when the Jews still lived in Palestine. Since then there have been no more. And yet: hadn't people told with good reason of strange deeds of the rabbi of Kluczýsk? Hadn't he made blind people see and saved the lame? How was it with Nathan Piczenik's daughter? She had been mad. They brought her to Kluczýsk. The rabbi looked at her. He said his words. Then he spat three times. And Piczenik's daughter went home free, light and rational. Other people have luck, thought Deborah. For miracles one also has to have luck. Mendel Singer's children have no luck! They're a teacher's children!

"If you were a reasonable man," she said to Mendel, "you would go to Kluczýsk tomorrow and ask the rabbi for advice." "I?" asked Mendel. "Why should I go to your rabbi? You were there once, go again! You believe in him, he will give you advice. You know that I think nothing of all that. No Jew needs an intermediary to the Lord. He hears our prayers if we do nothing unrighteous. But if we do something unrighteous, He can punish us!"

"Why is He punishing us now? Have we done wrong? Why is He so cruel?"

"You blaspheme Him, Deborah, leave me in peace, I can't talk with you any longer." And Mendel buried himself in a pious book.

Deborah reached for her shawl and went out. Outside stood Miriam. She stood there, reddened by the setting sun, in a white dress that now shimmered orange, with her smooth, shiny black hair, and looked straight into the setting sun with her large black eyes, which she held wide open, though the sun must have blinded them. She is beautiful, thought Deborah, I was once that beautiful, as beautiful as my daughter – what has become of me? I have become Mendel Singer's wife. Miriam is going with a Cossack, she is beautiful, perhaps she is right.

Miriam seemed not to see her mother. She observed with passionate concentration the glowing sun, which was now about to sink behind a heavy violet bank of clouds. For a few days this dark mass had stood every evening in the west, had portended storm and rain and had disappeared again the next day. Miriam had noticed that, at the moment the sun went down, over there in the cavalry barracks the soldiers began to sing, a whole *sotnia* began to sing, always the same song: *polyubil ya tebya za tvoyu krasotu.* Their duty was done, the Cossacks greeted the evening. Miriam repeated, humming, the lyrics of the song, of which she knew only the first two verses: I've fallen in love with you, because of your beauty. The song of a whole *sotnia* was meant for her! A hundred men were singing to her. Half an hour later she was meeting one of them, or even two. Sometimes three came.

She caught sight of her mother, remained standing calmly, knew that Deborah would come over. For weeks her mother no longer dared call Miriam. It was as if part of the terror that surrounded the Cossacks emanated from Miriam herself, as if the daughter already stood under the protection of the strange and wild barracks.

No, Deborah no longer called Miriam. Deborah came to Miriam. Deborah, in an old shawl, stood old, ugly, anxious before the gold-gleaming Miriam, stopped at the edge of the wooden sidewalk, as if she were following an old law that commanded ugly mothers to stand half a verst lower than beautiful daughters. "Your father is angry, Miriam!" said Deborah. "Let him be angry," replied Miriam, "your Mendel Singer."

For the first time Deborah heard the name of the father from the mouth of one of her children. For a moment it seemed to her that a stranger was speaking, not Mendel's child. A stranger – why should she say "Father"? Deborah wanted to turn around, she had made a mistake, she had spoken to a stranger. She began to turn. "Stay!" commanded Miriam – and it struck Deborah for the first time how hard her daughter's voice was. "A copper voice," thought Deborah. It sounded like one of the detested and feared church bells.

"Stay here, Mother!" repeated Miriam, "leave him alone, your husband, come with me to America. Leave Mendel Singer and Menuchim, the idiot, here."

"I've asked him to go to the rabbi, he refuses. I'm not going alone again to Kluczýsk. I'm afraid! He has already forbidden me once to leave Menuchim, even if his illness should last for years. What should I tell him, Miriam? Should I tell him that we have to leave on your account, because you, because you ––– "

"Because I run around with Cossacks," Miriam completed, without moving. And she went on: "Tell him what you please, it won't matter to me at all. In America I'll do what I want all the more. Because you married a Mendel Singer, I don't have to marry one too. Do you have a better man for me, huh? Do you have a dowry for your daughter?"

Miriam didn't raise her voice, even her questions didn't sound like questions, it was as if she were saying unimportant things, as if she were giving information about the prices of greens and eggs. "She is right," thought Deborah. "Help, dear God, she is right."

Deborah called all the good spirits to her aid. For she felt that she had to admit that her daughter was right, she herself spoke out of her daughter. Deborah began to be afraid of herself as much as she had been afraid of Miriam a short while ago. Threatening things were happening. The song of the soldiers wafted incessantly over. A small streak of the red sun still shone above the violet.

"I have to go," said Miriam, separated from the wall against which she had been leaning, light as a white butterfly she fluttered from the sidewalk, walked with quick coquettish feet along the middle of the road, out toward the barracks, toward the calling song of the Cossacks.

Fifty paces from the barracks, in the middle of the little path between the great forest and Sameshkin's grain, she waited for Ivan. "We're going to America," said Miriam.

"You won't forget me," Ivan admonished. "At this hour, when the sun goes down, you'll always think of me and not the others. And perhaps, with God's help, I'll follow you, you'll write to me. Pavel will read me your letters, don't write too many secret things between the two of us, or else I'll be ashamed." He kissed Miriam, strongly and many times, his kisses rattled like shots through the evening. A devilish girl, he thought, now she's going away, to America, I have to find another. No one else is as beautiful as she, four more years I have to serve. He was tall, strong as a bear and shy. His gigantic hands trembled when he was to touch a girl. And he was not at home in love, Miriam had taught him everything, what ideas had she not already had!

They embraced, as they had yesterday and the day before, in the middle of the field, embedded among the fruits of the earth, surrounded and overarched by the heavy grain. The stalks lay down willingly when Miriam and Ivan sank to the ground; even before they sank, the stalks seemed to lie down. Today their love was fiercer, briefer and, so to speak, frightened. It was as if Miriam already had to go to America tomorrow. The parting already trembled in their love. As they merged together, they were already far apart, separated from each other by the ocean. How good, thought Miriam, that he's not the one leaving, that I'm not the one staying behind. They lay for a long time exhausted, helpless, mute, as if they were seriously wounded. A thousand thoughts reeled through their brains. They didn't notice the rain that had finally come. It had begun gently and sneakily, it was a long time before its drops were heavy enough to break through the dense golden enclosure of stalks. Suddenly they were at the mercy of the pouring water. They awoke, began to run. The rain confused them, transformed the world completely, deprived them of their sense of time. They thought it was already late, they listened for the bells from the tower, but only the rain roared, heavier and heavier, all the other voices of the night were uncannily hushed. They kissed each other on their wet faces, squeezed each other's hands, water was between them, neither could feel the body of the other. Hastily they said goodbye, their ways parted, already Ivan was enveloped and invisible in the rain. Never again will I see him! thought Miriam, as she ran home. The harvest is coming. Tomorrow the peasants will be frightened, because one rain brings others.

She arrived home, waited awhile under the overhang as if it were possible to get dry in a short minute. She decided to enter the room. It was dark, everyone was already asleep. She lay down softly, wet as she was, she let her clothes dry on her body and didn't move. Outside the rain roared. Everyone knew already that Mendel was going to America, one pupil after another stopped coming to the lessons. Now there were only five boys left, and they didn't come at regular times either. The papers Kapturak had not yet brought, the ship tickets Sam had not yet sent. But the house of Mendel Singer already began to decay. How rotten it must have been, thought Mendel. It has been rotten, and we haven't known it. He who cannot pay attention is like a deaf man, and is worse off than a deaf man – so it is written somewhere. Here my grandfather was a teacher; here my father was a teacher, here I was a teacher. Now I am going to America. My son Jonas the Cossacks have taken, Miriam they want to take from me too. Menuchim – what will become of Menuchim?

On the evening of that same day he visited the Billes family. It was a happy family, it seemed to Mendel Singer that they had much undeserved luck; all the daughters were married, down to the youngest, to whom he now wanted to offer his house, all three sons had escaped the military and gone out into the world, one to Hamburg, another to California, the third to Paris. It was a happy family, God's hand rested over it, it lay cozily bedded in God's broad hand. Old Billes was always cheerful. Mendel Singer had taught all his sons. Old Billes had been a pupil of the old Singer. Because they had already known each other so long, Mendel believed he had a small right to the luck of the strangers.

The Billes family – they did not live in affluence – was pleased with Mendel Singer's proposal. Good! – the young couple will take over the house and Menuchim with it. "He's no work at all," said Mendel Singer. "And he does better from year to year. Soon, with God's help, he will be healthy. Then my older son, Shemariah, will come over or he will send someone and bring Menuchim to America."

"And what do you hear from Jonas?" asked old Billes. Mendel hadn't heard anything for a long time from his Cossack, as he inwardly called him – not without contempt, but also not without pride. Nonetheless, he answered: "Nothing but good things! He's learned to read and write, and he has been promoted. If he weren't a Jew, who knows, maybe he'd already be an officer!" It was impossible for Mendel to stand there in the face of this lucky family with the heavy burden of his great misfortune on his back. That's why he stretched his back and feigned a bit of joy.

It was arranged that Mendel Singer would turn over the use of his house to the Billes family before simple witnesses, not before officials, because that cost money. Three or four respectable Jews sufficed as witnesses. In the meantime Mendel got an advance of thirty rubles, because his pupils no longer came and the money at home was running out.

A week later Kapturak rolled once again in his small light yellow wagon through the little town. Everything was there: the money, the ship tickets, the passports, the visa, the head tax for each of them and even the fee for Kapturak. "A punctual payer," said Kapturak. "Your son Shemariah, known as Sam, is a punctual payer. A gentleman, they say over there . . . "

Kapturak would accompany the Singer family as far as the border. In four weeks the steamer "Neptune" was leaving from Bremen to New York.

The Billes family came to take inventory. The bedding, six

pillows, six sheets, six red and blue checkered covers Deborah was taking along, they were leaving behind the straw sacks and the sparse bedding for Menuchim.

Though Deborah didn't have much to pack, and though she kept in her head everything she possessed, she nonetheless remained incessantly active. She packed, she unpacked again. She counted the dishes and counted them again. Menuchim broke two plates. He seemed on the whole to be gradually losing his stupid calm. He called his mother more often than usual, the only word he'd been able to speak for years he repeated, even when the mother wasn't near him, a dozen times. He was an idiot, that Menuchim! An idiot! How easy it is to say that! But who can say what a storm of fears and anxieties Menuchim's soul had to endure in those days, Menuchim's soul, which God had hidden in the impenetrable garb of stupidity! Yes, he was afraid, Menuchim the cripple! Sometimes he crawled on his own out of his corner to the door, crouched on the threshold in the sun like a sick dog and squinted at the passersby, seeming to see only their boots and pants, their stockings and coats. Sometimes he reached unexpectedly for his mother's apron and grumbled. Deborah picked him up, though he already weighed a considerable amount. Nonetheless, she rocked him in her arms and sang two or three fragmented verses of a nursery rhyme that she herself had already completely forgotten and that began to reawaken in her memory as soon as she felt her unfortunate son in her arms. Then she let him crouch on the floor again, and went back to work, which for days had consisted entirely of packing and counting. Suddenly she stopped again. She stood still for a while with pensive eyes, which were not unlike Menuchim's; so without life were they, so helplessly searching in an unknown distance for the thoughts that the brain refused to provide. Her foolish gaze fell on the sack into which the pillows would be sewn. Perhaps, it occurred to her, they could sew Menuchim into a sack? Immediately she trembled at the idea that the customs officers would stick long sharp spears through the passengers' sacks. And she began to unpack again, and the decision to stay flashed through her mind, as the rabbi of Kluczýsk had said: "Do not leave him, as if he were a healthy child!" The strength that belonged to faith she could no longer muster, and gradually she was also abandoned by the powers that a person needs to endure despair.

It was as if they, Deborah and Mendel, had not voluntarily made the decision to go to America, but rather as if America had come over them, set upon them, with Shemariah, Mac and Kapturak. Now that they realized it, it was too late. They could no longer escape from America. The papers came to them, the ship tickets, the head taxes. "What if," Deborah asked at one point, "Menuchim suddenly recovers, today or tomorrow?" Mendel shook his head for a while. Then he said: "If Menuchim recovers, we'll take him with us!" And both of them yielded silently to the hope that, tomorrow or the day after, Menuchim would stand up healthy from his bed, with strong limbs and perfect speech.

On Sunday they are to leave. Today is Thursday. For the last time Deborah stands before her stove to prepare the Sabbath meal, the white poppy-seed bread and the braided rolls. The open fire burns, hisses and crackles, and the smoke fills the room, as on every Thursday for thirty years. It's raining outside. The rain drives the smoke back out of the chimney, the old familiar jagged stain in the lime of the ceiling shows itself again in its damp freshness. For ten years the hole in the roof shingles should have been repaired, the Billes family will do it. The large ironbound brown suitcase stands packed with its sturdy iron bar over the slit and two gleaming new iron locks. Sometimes Menuchim crawls up to them and swings them. Then there's a merciless rattle, the locks strike against the iron bands and tremble for a long time and refuse to stand still. And the fire crackles, and the smoke fills the room.

On the Sabbath evening Mendel Singer took leave of his neighbors. They drank the yellowish green schnapps that someone had brewed himself and mixed with dry mushrooms. Thus the schnapps tastes not only strong, but also bitter. The farewell lasts longer than an hour. All wish Mendel luck. Some gaze at him doubtfully, some envy him. But all tell him that America is a glorious land. A Jew can wish for nothing better than to reach America.

That night Deborah left the bed and went, her hand carefully cupped around a candle, to Menuchim's pallet. He lay on his back, his heavy head was leaning on the rolled-up gray blanket, his eyelids were half open, one saw the white of his eyes. With each breath his body trembled, his sleeping fingers moved incessantly. He held his hands on his breast. In sleep his face was even paler and flabbier than during the day. His bluish lips were open, with white drops of foam in the corners of his mouth. Deborah extinguished the light. She crouched for a few seconds next to her son, rose and crept back into bed. Nothing will become of him, she thought, nothing will become of him. She didn't fall asleep again.

On Sunday, at eight o'clock in the morning, comes a messenger from Kapturak. It's the man with the blue cap who once brought Shemariah across the border. Today, too, the man with the blue cap remains standing at the door, declines to have tea, then wordlessly helps roll out the suitcase and puts it on the wagon. A comfortable wagon, there's room for four people. Their feet rest in soft hay, the wagon is redolent of the whole land in late summer. The backs of the horses shine, brushed and lustrous, brown curved mirrors. A broad yoke with many little silver bells spans their slender and haughty necks. Even though it's daylight, one sees the spraying sparks that their hooves strike from the gravel.

Once more Deborah holds Menuchim in her arms. The Billes family is already there, surrounds the wagon and doesn't stop talking. Mendel Singer sits on the coach box, and Miriam leans her back against her father's. Only Deborah is still standing outside the door with Menuchim the cripple in her arms.

Suddenly she parts from him. She sets him gently on the

threshold as one lays a corpse in a coffin, stands up, stretches, lets her tears flow, over her naked face naked tears. She is resolved. Her son is staying. She will go to America. No miracle has occurred.

Weeping, she climbs into the wagon. She doesn't see the faces of the people whose hands she squeezes. Her eyes are two great seas full of tears. She hears the clatter of the horses' hooves. She is leaving. She cries out, doesn't know she's crying out, the cry bursts from her, her heart has a mouth and cries. The wagon stops, she jumps out of it, light-footed as a youth. Menuchim is still sitting on the threshold. She falls down before Menuchim. "Mama, Mama!" babbles Menuchim. She remains lying.

The Billes family lifts Deborah up. She screams, she resists, she finally stays still. They carry her back to the wagon and lay her down on the hay. The wagon rolls very swiftly toward Dubno.

Six hours later they sat on the train, the slow passenger line, together with many unknown people. The train ran gently through the land, the meadows and the fields, on which people were harvesting, the peasant men and women, the huts and herds greeted the train. The soft song of the wheels lulled the passengers to sleep. Deborah hadn't yet spoken a word. She slumbered. The wheels of the train repeated incessantly, incessantly: Do not leave him! Do not leave him! Do not leave him!

Mendel Singer prayed. He prayed by heart and mechanically, he didn't think about the meaning of the words, their sound alone sufficed, God understood what they meant. Thus Mendel benumbed his great fear of the water on which he would find himself in a few days. Sometimes he cast an absentminded glance at Miriam. She sat opposite him, beside the man with the blue cap. Mendel didn't see how she snuggled up to the man. The man didn't speak to her, he was waiting for the short quarter of an hour between the fall of dusk and the moment the conductor would light the tiny gas flame. From this quarter of an hour and later from the night, when the gas flames would be extinguished again, the man with the blue cap was expecting all sorts of delights.

The next morning he took an indifferent leave of the old Singers, only Miriam's hand he squeezed with silent warmth. They were at the border. The officers took their passports. When they called Mendel's name he trembled. Without cause. Everything was in order. They crossed.

They boarded a new train, saw other stations, heard new bell signals, saw new uniforms. They journeyed for three days and changed trains twice. In the afternoon of the third day they arrived in Bremen. A man from the shipping company bellowed: "Mendel Singer." The Singer family presented itself. The official was expecting no less than nine families. He arranged them in a row, counted them three times, read out their names and gave each a number. Now they stood there and didn't know what to do with the metal tags. The official went away. He had promised to come back soon. But the nine families, twenty-five people, didn't move. They stood in a row on the platform, the metal tags in their hands, their bundles at their feet. At the farthest corner to the left, because he had announced himself so late, stood Mendel Singer.

During the whole journey he'd spoken scarcely a word with his wife and daughter. Both women had been silent too. But now Deborah seemed unable to bear the silence any longer. "Why aren't you moving?" asked Deborah. "No one is moving," replied Mendel. "Why don't you ask the people?" "No one is asking." "What are we waiting for?" "I don't know what we're waiting for." "Do you think I can sit down on the suitcase?" "Sit down on the suitcase."

But the moment Deborah had spread her skirts to sit down, the official from the shipping company appeared and announced in Russian, Polish, German and Yiddish that he now intended to escort all nine families to the port; that he would put them in a shack for the night; and that tomorrow at seven in the morning the "Neptune" would weigh anchor.

In the shack they lay, in Bremerhaven, the metal tags tight in their balled fists, even while they were asleep. From the snoring of the twenty-five and from the movements each made on the hard beds, the beams trembled and the little yellow electric bulbs swung softly. It had been forbidden to make tea. With dry palates they had gone to sleep. Only Miriam had been offered red candies by a Polish barber. With a large sticky ball in her mouth Miriam fell asleep.

At five o'clock in the morning Mendel awoke. He climbed laboriously out of the wooden container in which he had slept, looked for the water faucet, went outside to see where the east lay. Then he returned, stood in a corner and prayed. He whispered to himself, but as he whispered, a loud pain seized him, clawed into his heart and tore at it so fiercely that Mendel heaved a loud groan in the midst of whispering. A few sleepers awoke, looked down and smiled at the Jew who hopped and wobbled in the corner, rocked his upper body forward and back, and performed a miserable dance to the glory of God.

Mendel wasn't yet finished when the official flung open the door. A sea breeze had blown him into the shack. "Everybody up!" he cried a few times and in all the languages of the world.

It was still early when they reached the ship. They were permitted to cast a few glances into the dining rooms of the first and second class before they were pushed into the steerage. Mendel Singer didn't move. He stood on the highest step of a narrow iron ladder, at his back the port, the land, the continent, his home, the past. To his left beamed the sun. White was the ship. Green was the water. A sailor came and commanded Mendel Singer to leave the step. He placated the sailor with a hand motion. He was completely calm and without fear. He cast a fleeting glance at the sea and drank consolation from the endlessness of the choppy water. It was eternal. Mendel was aware that God himself had created it. He had poured it out of His inexhaustible secret wellspring. Now it rolled between the solid lands. Deep down on its bottom coiled Leviathan, the holy fish, whom the pious and righteous will eat on the Day of Judgment. "Neptune" was the name of the ship on which Mendel stood. It was a large ship. But compared with the Leviathan and with the sea, with the sky and with the wisdom of the Eternal, it was a tiny ship. No, Mendel felt no fear. He mollified the sailor, he, a little black Jew on a gigantic ship and before the eternal ocean, he turned again in a semicircle and murmured the blessing that is to be spoken at the sight of the sea. He turned in a semicircle and scattered the individual words of the blessing over the green waves: "Praised are you, Eternal One, our Lord, who created the seas and with them divides the continents!"

At that moment the sirens sounded. The engines began to rumble. And the air and the ship and the people trembled. Only the sky remained still and blue, blue and still.

IX

The fourteenth evening of the voyage was illuminated by the great fiery balls shot by the lightships. "Now," said a Jew, who had already made this journey twice, to Mendel Singer, "the Statue of Liberty appears. It's a hundred and fifty feet tall, hollow inside, you can climb it. Around her head she's wearing a crown of light. In her right hand she's holding a torch. And the best part is that this torch burns at night and yet can never burn out. Because it's only lit electrically. That's the sort of trick they do in America."

The morning of the fifteenth day they were unloaded. Deborah,

Miriam and Mendel stood close together, because they were afraid of losing one another.

Men in uniform came, they seemed to Mendel Singer a little dangerous, even though they had no sabers. Some wore sparkling white garments and looked half like gendarmes and half like angels. These are the Cossacks of America, thought Mendel Singer, and he watched his daughter Miriam.

They were called according to the alphabet, each received his luggage, no one stuck sharp spears through it. Perhaps we could have taken Menuchim with us, thought Deborah.

Suddenly Shemariah stood before them.

All three of them were startled in the same way.

They saw simultaneously their little old house again, the old Shemariah and the new Shemariah, known as Sam.

They saw Shemariah and Sam at the same time, as if a Sam had been pulled over a Shemariah, a transparent Sam.

It was indeed Shemariah, but it was Sam.

There were two of them. The one wore a black cap, a black robe and high boots, and the first downy little black hairs sprouted from the pores of his cheeks.

The second wore a light gray coat, a snow-white cap like that of the captain, wide yellow pants, a bright shirt of green silk, and his face was smooth, like an noble gravestone.

The second was almost Mac.

The first spoke with his old voice – they heard only the voice, not the words.

The second slapped his father on the shoulder with a strong hand and said, and they only now heard the words: "Hello, old chap!" – and understood nothing.

The first was Shemariah. But the second was Sam.

First Sam kissed his father, then his mother, then Miriam. All three sniffed Sam's shaving soap, which smelled of snowdrops and also a little like carbolic acid. It reminded them of a garden and at the same time of a hospital.

Inwardly they repeated to themselves a few times that Sam was Shemariah. Only then were they happy. "All the others," said Sam, "go into quarantine. Not you! Mac arranged it. He has two cousins who are employed here."

Half an hour later Mac appeared.

He still looked exactly as he had when he had appeared in the little town. Broad, loud, ranting in an incomprehensible language and his pockets already bulging with sweet cookies, which he immediately began to hand out and to eat himself. A bright red tie fluttered like a flag over his chest.

"You have to go into quarantine after all," said Mac. For he had exaggerated. His cousins were indeed employed in this area, but only in the customs inspection. "But I'll accompany you. Don't worry!"

They actually didn't need to worry. Mac shouted at all the officials that Miriam was his bride and Mendel and Deborah his parents-in-law.

Every afternoon at three o'clock Mac came to the fence of the camp. He stuck his hand through the wires, even though it was forbidden, and greeted them all. After four days he managed to free the Singer family. How he managed it he did not reveal. For it was one of Mac's qualities that he told with great enthusiasm things he had made up; and that he kept things secret that had really occurred.

He insisted that they view America thoroughly on a wagon belonging to his firm, before they went home.

He took Mendel Singer, Deborah and Miriam on a tour.

It was a bright and hot day. Mendel and Deborah sat facing forward, Miriam, Mac and Sam opposite them. The heavy wagon clattered through the streets with a furious power, as it seemed to Mendel Singer, as if it intended to shatter stone and asphalt for eternity and shake the houses to their foundations. The leather seat burned under Mendel's body like a hot stove. Even though they stayed in the dark shade of the high walls, the heat blazed like gray melting lead through the old cap of black silk rep on Mendel's head, penetrated into his brain and soldered it up, with damp, sticky, painful intensity. Since his arrival he had scarcely slept, eaten little and drunk almost nothing at all. He was wearing his native rubber galoshes over his heavy boots and his feet were burning as in an open fire. Tightly clamped between his knees he had his umbrella, the wooden handle of which was hot and couldn't be touched, as if it were made of red iron. Before Mendel's eyes wafted a densely woven veil of soot, dust and heat. He thought of the desert through which his ancestors had wandered for forty years. But they had at least gone on foot, he said to himself. The mad haste in which they were now racing along aroused a wind, but it was a hot wind, the fiery breath of hell. Instead of cooling, it blazed. The wind was no wind, it consisted of din and noise, it was a wafting din. It was made up of the shrill ringing of a hundred invisible bells, of the dangerous, metallic roar of the trains, of the blaring calls of countless trumpets, of the beseeching screech of the tracks at the curves of the streets, of the bellowing of Mac, who explained America to his passengers through an overpowering megaphone, of the murmur of the people all around, of the raucous laughter of a strange fellow passenger behind Mendel's back, of the incessant talk that Sam flung into his father's face, talk that Mendel didn't understand, but at which he constantly nodded, a fearful and simultaneously friendly smile around his lips like a painful clamp of iron.

Even if he'd had the courage to remain earnest, as befitted his situation, he wouldn't have been able to remove the smile. He didn't have the strength to change his expression. The muscles of his face were paralyzed. He would rather have wept like a small child. He smelled the sharp tar from the melting asphalt, the dry and desiccated dust in the air, the rancid and greasy stink from sewers and cheese shops, the acrid smell of onions, the sickly-sweet gasoline smoke of the cars, the putrid swamp smell from fish halls, the lilies of the valley and the carbolic acid from the cheeks of his son. All the smells mingled in a hot vapor that struck him, along with the noise that filled his ears and wanted to burst his skull. Soon he no longer knew what was to be heard, to be seen, to be smelled. He was still smiling and nodding his head. America besieged him, America broke him, America shattered him. After a few minutes he fainted.

He awoke in a lunchroom to which they'd brought him in a hurry to refresh him. In a round mirror wreathed with a hundred little light bulbs he glimpsed his white beard and his bony nose and thought in the first instant that the beard and nose belonged to someone else. Only by his family members, who surrounded him, did he recognize himself. He felt a little ashamed. He opened his lips with some effort and apologized to his son. Mac grasped his hand and shook it as if he were congratulating Mendel Singer on a successful trick or a winning bet. Around the mouth of the old man the iron clamp of the smile settled again, and the unknown power moved his head again, so that it looked as if Mendel Singer were nodding. He saw Miriam. She had tousled black hair under her yellow shawl, some soot on her pale cheeks and a long straw between her teeth. Deborah sat, broad, silent, with flared nostrils and heaving breasts, on a round chair without a back. It looked as if she would soon fall.

What do these people have to do with me? thought Mendel. What does all of America have to do with me? My son, my wife, my daughter, this Mac? Am I still Mendel Singer? Is this still my family? Am I still Mendel Singer? Where is my son Menuchim?

He felt as if he had been cast out of himself, he would have to live separated from himself from now on. He felt as if he had left himself behind in Zuchnow, near Menuchim. And as his lips smiled and his head nodded, his heart began slowly to freeze, it pounded like a metal drumstick against cold glass. Already he was lonely, Mendel Singer: already he was in America . . .

Part Two

X

A few hundred years earlier an ancestor of Mendel Singer had probably come from Spain to Volhynia. He had a more fortunate, more ordinary, in any case less noticed fate than did his descendant, and as a result we don't know whether it took him many or few years to settle into the strange land. But of Mendel Singer we know that he was at home in New York after a few months.

Yes, he was almost at home in America! He already knew that "old chap" meant father in American and "old fool" mother, or the other way around. He knew a few businessmen from the Bowery with whom his son associated, Essex Street, where he lived, and Houston Street, where his son's department store was, his son Sam. He knew that Sam was already an "American boy," that one said "goodbye," "how do you do" and "please," if one was a refined man, that a merchant from Grand Street could demand respect and sometimes might live on the river, on that river for which Shemariah too yearned. He had been told that America was "God's own country," as Palestine once had been, and New York actually "the miracle city," as Jerusalem once had been. Praying, however, was called "service," and so was charity. Sam's small son, born scarcely a week after his grandfather's arrival, is named nothing less than MacLincoln and in some years, whoosh goes the time in America, will be a "college boy." "My dear boy," the daughter-in-law calls the little one these days. She is still named Vega, strangely enough. She's blond and gentle, with blue eyes that reveal to Mendel Singer more goodness than intelligence. Let her be dumb! Women need no intellect, God help her, amen! Between twelve and two it's time to eat "lunch," and between six and eight "dinner." Mendel doesn't observe these times. He eats at three in the afternoon and at ten at night, as at home, even though it's actually day at home when he sits down to his evening meal, or perhaps early morning, who knows. "All right" means agreed, and to give assent one says "yes!" If one wants to wish someone something good, one wishes him not happiness and health, but "prosperity." In the near future Sam already intends to rent a new apartment, on the river, with a "parlor." He already owns a gramophone, Miriam borrows it sometimes from her sister-in-law and carries it in faithful arms through the streets, as if it were a sick child. The gramophone can play many waltzes, but also Kol Nidre. Sam washes twice a day; the suit he sometimes wears in the evening he calls "dress." Deborah has already been to the movies ten times and to the theater three times. She has a dark gray silk dress. Sam gave it to her. She wears a great golden necklace around her neck, she's reminiscent of one of the women of pleasure who are sometimes mentioned in the holy scriptures. Miriam is a salesgirl in Sam's store. She comes home after midnight and leaves again at seven in the morning. She says: Good evening, Father! Good morning, Father! and nothing more. Here and there Mendel Singer hears from conversations, which stream past his ears as a river flows past the feet of an old man who stands on the bank, that Mac goes walking, dancing, swimming, exercising with Miriam. He knows, Mendel Singer, that Mac is not a Jew, the Cossacks aren't Jews either, it's hasn't yet gone that far, God will help, we will see. Deborah and Miriam are living well together. Peace is in the house. Mother and daughter whisper to each other, often, long after midnight, Mendel pretends to sleep. He can do it easily. He sleeps in the kitchen, wife and daughter sleep in the only living area. One doesn't dwell in palaces in America either. One lives on the second floor! A stroke of luck. How easily they might have lived on the third, on the fourth, on the fifth! The staircase is steep and dirty, always dark. One illuminates the steps with matches even during the day. It smells, warm, damp and sticky, of cats. But sourdough with rodent poison and glass shards ground into it still has to be put in the corners each evening. Deborah scrubs the floor each week, but it's never as saffron-yellow as at home. Why is that? Is Deborah too weak? Is she too lazy? Is she too old? All the boards squeak when Mendel walks through the room. Impossible to tell where Deborah now hides the money. Sam gives ten dollars a week. Nonetheless Deborah is indignant. She's a woman, occasionally something gets into her. She has a good gentle daughter-in-law, but Deborah claims that Vega wallows in luxury. When Mendel hears that sort of talk he says: "Be silent, Deborah! Be content with the children! Are you still not old enough to be silent? Are you no longer able to reproach me for earning too little and does it torment you that you can't quarrel with me? Shemariah brought us here so that we can grow old and die near him. His wife honors us both, as is proper. What more do you want, Deborah?"

She didn't know exactly what she was missing. Perhaps she had hoped to find in America a completely foreign world, in which it would have been possible to forget immediately the old life and Menuchim. But this America was no new world. There were more Jews here than in Kluczýsk, it was actually a larger Kluczýsk. Had it been necessary to take the long journey across the great water to arrive again in Kluczýsk, which they could have reached in Sameshkin's cart? The windows faced a dark light-well in which cats, rats and children scuffled, at three in the afternoon, even in spring, the petroleum lamp had to be lit, there wasn't even electric light, they didn't yet have their own gramophone either. At home Deborah at least had light and sun. Certainly! She went now and then with her daughter-in-law to the movies, she had already taken the subway twice, Miriam was a noble young lady, with a hat and silk stockings. She'd become good. She even earned money. Mac was running around with her, better Mac than the Cossacks. He was Shemariah's best friend. They didn't understand a word of his incessant talking, but they'd get used to it. He was more capable than ten Jews, and also certainly had the advantage of not demanding a dowry. Ultimately it was another world after all. An American Mac was no Russian Mac. Deborah couldn't make ends meet here either. Life rapidly became more expensive, she couldn't stop saving, the usual floorboard already concealed eighteen and a half dollars, the carrots decreased, the eggs became hollow, the potatoes frozen, the soups watery, the carp thin and the pike short, the ducks meager, the geese tough, and the chickens nothing.

No, she didn't know exactly what she was missing, she missed Menuchim. Often, while asleep, awake, shopping, at the movies, cleaning, baking, she heard him calling. Mama! Mama! he called. The only word he had learned to say he now must have already forgotten. She heard strange children call Mama, the mothers answered, not a single mother voluntarily parted from her child. They shouldn't have gone to America. But they could still return home!

"Mendel," she sometimes said, "shouldn't we go back, see Menuchim?"

"And the money, and the journey, and live on what? Do you think that Shemariah can give so much? He's a good son, but he's not Vanderbilt. Maybe it was fated. Let's stay for the time being! Menuchim we'll see here, if he should recover."

Nonetheless the thought of leaving was fixed in Mendel Singer and never left him. Once, when he visited his son in the store (he sat in the office behind the glass door and saw the customers coming and going and inwardly blessed everyone who entered), he said to Shemariah: "We still hear nothing of Menuchim. In the last letter from Billes there wasn't a word about him. What would you think if I went over to see him?" Shemariah, known as Sam, was an American boy, he said: "Father, that's impractical. If it were possible to bring Menuchim here, he'd recover immediately. American medicine is the best in the world, I just read that in the newspaper. They cure such illnesses with injections, simply with injections! But since we can't bring him here, poor Menuchim, why spend the money? I don't want to say that it's completely impossible! But just now, when Mac and I are preparing a really big business venture and money is tight, we don't want to talk about it! Wait another few weeks! Between you and me: Mac and I, we're now speculating in building sites. We've just had an old house on Delancey Street torn down. I tell you, Father, tearing down is almost as expensive as building up. But one shouldn't complain! We're doing better! When I think of how we started with insurance! Up and down the stairs! And now we have this business, you can already say: this department store! Now the insurance agents come to me. I look at them, think to myself: I know the business, and throw them out, personally. I throw them all out!"

Mendel Singer didn't quite comprehend why Sam threw out the agents and why he was so pleased about it. Sam felt that, and said: "Do you want to have breakfast with me, Father?" He was acting as if he'd forgotten that his father ate only at home, he gladly seized the opportunity to emphasize the distance separating him from the customs of his homeland, he slapped his forehead as if he were Mac, and said:

"Oh, yes! I forgot! But you'll eat a banana, Father!" And he had a banana brought to his father. "About Miriam," he resumed, in the midst of eating, "she's doing well. She's the most beautiful girl here in the store. If she were working for a stranger, she'd have been offered a job as a model long ago. But I wouldn't want my sister to lend her figure to strange clothes. And Mac doesn't want it either!" He waited to see whether his father would say something about Mac. But Mendel Singer was silent. He wasn't suspicious. He had scarcely heard the last sentence. He abandoned himself to his deep admiration for his children, especially for Shemariah. How clever he was, how quickly he thought, how fluently he spoke English, how he could press bell pushes, bawl out errand boys, he was a boss.

He went into the shirts and ties department to see his daughter. "Good day, Father!" she called, in the midst of serving someone. She showed him respect, at home it had been different. She probably didn't love him, but it wasn't written: Love thy father and mother! but: Honor thy father and mother! He nodded to her and left again. He went home. He was calm, he walked slowly in the middle of the street, greeted the neighbors, took pleasure in the children. He still wore his cap of black silk rep and the half-long caftan and the high boots. But the skirts of his coat no longer knocked with a hasty wing-beat against the rawhide shafts. For in America, where everything hurried, Mendel Singer had first learned to walk slowly. Thus he walked through time toward old age, from the morning prayer to the evening prayer, from breakfast to dinner, from awakening to sleep. In the afternoon, at the hour when his pupils had come at home, he lay down on the horsehair sofa, slept an hour and dreamed of Menuchim. Then he read the newspaper a bit. Then he went to the shop of the Skovronnek family, where gramophones, records, music books and song lyrics were sold, played and sung. All the older people of the neighborhood gathered there. They spoke about politics and told anecdotes from the old country. Sometimes, when it had grown late, they went to the Skovronneks' living room and very quickly prayed an evening prayer.

On the way home, which Mendel sought to prolong a little, he abandoned himself to the idea that a letter was waiting for him at home. The letter said clearly and explicitly first: that Menuchim had grown completely healthy and rational; second: that Jonas had left the service due to a minor affliction and wanted to come to America. Mendel Singer knew that this letter had not yet come. But he tried, so to speak, to give the letter a favorable opportunity, so that it would wish to arrive. And with a softly pounding heart he rang the bell. The instant he glimpses Deborah it's over. The letter was not yet there. It will be an evening like every other.

One day, when he made a detour on his way home, he saw on the corner of the street an adolescent boy, who appeared familiar to him from a distance. The boy was leaning in a doorway and weeping. Mendel heard a thin whimper; as soft as it was, it reached Mendel on the opposite side of the street. Mendel recognized this sound. He stopped. He decided to approach the boy, ask him what was wrong, console him. He started toward him. Suddenly the whimper grew louder, Mendel faltered in the middle of the street. In the shadow of the evening and the doorway in which the boy was crouching, he seemed to take on Menuchim's outline and posture. Yes, thus, on the threshold of his house in Zuchnow, had Menuchim crouched and whimpered. Mendel took a few more steps. Then the boy scurried into the house. Mendel walked up to the door. The dark hallway had already swallowed the boy.

Even more slowly than before Mendel went home.

It wasn't Deborah who came to the door when he rang, but his son Sam. Mendel remained at the threshold for a moment. Even though he had been prepared for nothing but a pleasurable surprise, fear seized him, a misfortune might have occurred. Yes, his heart was so accustomed to misfortune that he still became frightened, even after a long preparation for good luck. What joyful surprise, he thought, can befall a man like me? Everything sudden is evil, and the good creeps slowly.

But Shemariah's voice soon calmed him. "Come in!" said Sam. He pulled his father by the hand into the room. Deborah had lit two lamps. His daughter-in-law Vega, Miriam and Mac were sitting around the table. The whole house seemed to Mendel to have changed. The two lamps – they were of the same kind – looked like twins, and they illuminated the room less than they did each other. It was as if they were laughing at each other, one lamp at the other, and that cheered Mendel especially. "Sit down, Father!" said Sam. He wasn't curious, Mendel, he already feared that one of those American stories was now coming, which made the whole world joyful and in which he could find no pleasure. What will have happened? he thought. They will have given me a gramophone. Or they've decided to celebrate a wedding. He sat down very awkwardly. All were silent. Then Sam said – and it was as if he were lighting a third lamp in the room: "Father, we've earned fifteen thousand dollars at one stroke."

Mendel rose and offered everyone present his hand. He came to Mac last. To him Mendel said: "I thank you." Sam immediately translated the three words into English. Mac now rose too and embraced Mendel. Then he began to speak. He didn't stop again. For the rest of the evening no one spoke but Mac. Deborah began converting the sum into rubles and didn't finish. Vega thought of new furniture in the new apartment, especially of a piano. Her son should take piano lessons. Mendel thought of a trip home. Miriam only heard Mac talking and strained to understand as much as possible. Because she didn't understand his language, she believed that Mac spoke too cleverly to be understood. Sam wondered whether he should put all the money into his department store. Only Mac thought little, didn't worry, made no plans. He said what came to his mind.

The next day they went to Atlantic City. "Beautiful nature!"

said Deborah. Mendel saw only the water. And he remembered that wild night at home when he had lain with Sameshkin in the roadside ditch. And he heard the chirping of the crickets and the croaking of the frogs. "At home," he said suddenly, "the earth is as wide as the water in America." He hadn't wanted to say that at all. "Do you hear what your father is saying?" Deborah declared. "He's getting old!"

Yes, yes, I'm getting old, thought Mendel.

When they returned home, there was a thick, bulging letter in the crack of the door, which the mailman hadn't been able to push through. "You see," said Mendel, bending down, "this letter is a good letter. The good luck has begun. One stroke of luck brings another, praised be God. May he help us further."

It was a letter from the Billes family. And it was indeed a good letter. It contained the news that Menuchim had suddenly begun to talk.

"Dr. Soltysiuk has seen him," wrote the Billes family. "He couldn't believe it. They want to send Menuchim to Petersburg, the great doctors want to rack their brains over him. One day, it was Thursday afternoon, he was home alone, and there was a fire in the stove, like every Thursday, a burning log fell out, and now the whole floor is burnt, and the walls have to be lime-washed. It costs a pretty little sum. Menuchim ran into the street, he can also run quite well now, and cried: 'It's burning!' And since then he can say a few words.

Too bad, though, that it was a week after Jonas's departure. For your Jonas was here, on furlough, he is really already a great soldier, and he didn't even know that you are in America. He writes to you here too, on the other side."

Mendel turned the page over and read:

Dear Father, dear mother, dear brother and dear sister!

So you're in America, it struck me like lightning. It's actually my fault, because I never, or, I recall, only once, wrote to you, but still, as I said, it struck me like lightning. Don't worry about it. I'm doing very well. Everyone is good to me, and I'm good to everyone. I'm especially good to the horses. I can ride like the best Cossack and pick up a handkerchief from the ground with my teeth at a gallop. I love such things, and the military too. I will stay, even when I've completed my service. Here you're provided for, you have food, everything that's necessary is ordered from above, you don't need to think yourself. I don't know whether I'm writing it in a way that you can completely understand. Maybe you can't understand it at all. In the stable it's very warm, and I love horses. If one of you should come over at some point, you could see me. My captain has said that if I remain such a good soldier, I can petition the Tsar, that is, his noble Majesty, so that my brother's desertion is forgiven and forgotten. That would be my greatest joy, to see Shemariah again in this life, we grew up together after all.

Sameshkin sends his greetings, he's doing well. People here sometimes say that a war is going to come. If it should really come,

*you have to be prepared for me to die, just as I am prepared for it,
because I am a soldier.*

*In case that should happen I embrace you once and for all and
forever. But don't be sad, perhaps I will stay alive.*

Your son Jonas

Mendel Singer took off his glasses, saw that Deborah was
weeping and grasped her two hands for the first time in long
years. He drew her hands away from her tear-streaked face and
said almost solemnly: "Well, Deborah, the Lord has helped us.
Take your shawl, go down and bring a bottle of mead."

They sat at the table and drank the mead from tea glasses,
looked at each other and thought the same thing. "The Rabbi
is right," said Deborah. Her memory clearly dictated to her the
words that had long slept in her: "Pain will make him wise, ugliness kind, bitterness gentle, and illness strong."

"You never told me that," remarked Mendel.

"I'd forgotten it."

"We should have gone to Kluczýsk with Jonas too. He loves the
horses more than us."

"He's still young," Deborah consoled. "Maybe it's good that he
loves horses." And because she let no opportunity to be malicious
pass, she added: "He doesn't get the love of horses from you."

"No," said Mendel, smiling peaceably.

He began to think of returning home. Now they could perhaps

bring Menuchim to America soon. He lit a candle, extinguished the lamp and said: "Go to sleep, Deborah! When Miriam comes home, I'll show her the letter. I'm staying awake tonight." He took from the suitcase his old prayer book, it was at home in his hand, he opened to the psalms with a single stroke and sang one after another. The singing poured out of him. He had experienced grace and joy. Over him too arched God's broad vast kind hand. Sheltered by it and in honor of it he sang one psalm after another. The candle flickered in the soft but tireless wind, which Mendel's swaying upper body aroused. With his feet he beat time to the verses of the psalms. His heart rejoiced, and his body had to dance.

XI

Now the worries left the house of Mendel Singer for the first time. They had grown familiar to him, like detested siblings. He now turned fifty-nine years old. For fifty-eight years he had known them. The worries left him, death approached him. His beard was white, his eyes were weak. His back bent, and his hands trembled. His sleep was light, and the night was long. He wore contentment like strange borrowed clothing. His son moved into the area of the rich, Mendel remained on his street, in his apartment, with the blue petroleum lamps, in the neighborhood of the poor, the cats and the mice. He was pious, God-fearing and ordinary, an entirely everyday Jew. Few paid attention to him. Some didn't notice him at all. He visited a few old friends during the day: Menkes, the fruit seller, Skovronnek, the music shop owner, Rottenberg, the Bible scribe, Groschel, the shoemaker. His three children, his grandson and Mac came once a week. He had nothing at all to say to them. They told stories of the theater, of society and of politics. He listened and fell asleep. When Deborah woke him, he opened his eyes. "I wasn't asleep!" he assured them. Mac laughed. Sam smiled. Miriam whispered with Deborah. Mendel stayed awake for a while and nodded off again. He dreamed immediately: events from the old country and things he'd only heard about in America, theater, acrobats and dancers in gold and red, the President of the United States, the White House, the billionaire Vanderbilt and, again and again, Menuchim. The little cripple mingled with the red and gold of the singers, and before the pale radiance of the White House he clung as a poor gray blot. Mendel was too old to look at this and that with wakeful eyes. He took his children at their word that America was God's country, New York the city of miracles and English the most beautiful language. Americans were healthy, the American women beautiful, sports important, time precious, poverty a vice, wealth a merit, virtue half of success, belief in oneself the whole of it, dance hygienic, roller-skating a duty, charity an investment, anarchism a crime, strikers the enemies of mankind, agitators in league with the devil, modern machines blessings of heaven, Edison the greatest genius. Soon people will fly like birds, swim like fish, see the future like prophets, live in eternal peace and in perfect harmony build skyscrapers to the stars. The world will be very beautiful, thought Mendel, how lucky my grandson! He will live to see it all! Nonetheless, mingled with his admiration for the future was homesickness for Russia, and it calmed him to know that he would be a dead man before the triumphs of the living. He didn't know why. It calmed him. He was already too old for the new and too weak for triumphs. He had only one hope left: to see Menuchim. Sam or Mac would go over to fetch him. Perhaps Deborah would go too.

It was summer. The vermin in Mendel Singer's apartment multiplied unstoppably, even though the little brass wheels on the feet of the bed stood day and night in bowls full of petroleum and Deborah, with a soft chicken feather dipped in turpentine, brushed all the cracks in the furniture. The bedbugs crawled in long orderly rows down the walls, along the ceiling, waited in bloodthirsty malice for nightfall and fell onto the beds of the sleeping. The fleas jumped out of the black gaps between the floorboards into the clothes, onto the pillows, onto the blankets. The nights were hot and heavy. Through the open window came from time to time the distant roar of unknown trains, the brief regular thunder of a busy world stretching for miles and the murky haze from the neighbors' houses, dung heaps and open sewers. The cats made noise, the stray dogs howled, infants screamed through the night, and over Mendel Singer's head shuffled the footsteps of the sleepless, resounded the sneezes of those who had caught cold, meowed the weary in agonizing yawns. Mendel Singer lit the candle in the green bottle next to the bed and went to the window. There he saw the reddish reflection of the living American night, which was taking place somewhere, and the regular silver shadow of a searchlight that seemed to be desperately searching the night sky for God. Yes, and Mendel saw a few stars too, a few miserable stars, mutilated constellations. Mendel remembered the bright starry nights at home, the deep blue of the widely spanning sky, the gently curved sickle of the moon, the dark rustle of the pines in the forest, the voices of the crickets and frogs. It seemed to him that it would be easy now, as he was, to leave the house and wander on foot, the whole night, until he was again under the open sky and could hear the frogs and the crickets and Menuchim's whimper. Here, in America, that whimper joined the many voices in which the old country sang and spoke, along with the chirping of the crickets and the croaking of the frogs. Between them lay the ocean, thought Mendel. One had to board a ship, another ship, journey another twenty days and nights. Then he would be at home, with Menuchim.

The children urged him to finally leave the neighborhood. He was afraid. He didn't want to be rash. Now, when everything was beginning to go well, one didn't want to provoke God's wrath. When had things ever gone better for him? Why move to other areas? What good did that do? The few years in which he still intended to live he could spend in the company of the vermin.

He turned around. There slept Deborah. Once she had slept

here in the room with Miriam. Now Miriam lived with her brother. Or with Mac, thought Mendel, quickly and furtively. Deborah slept quietly, half covered, a broad smile on her broad face. What does she have to do with me? thought Mendel. Why are we still living together? Our desire is over, our children are grown and provided for, why am I with her? To eat what she has cooked! It is written that it's not good for a person to be alone. So we live together. For a very long time they had been living together, now it was a matter of who would die first. Probably I, thought Mendel. She is healthy and has few worries. She still hides money under some floorboard. She doesn't know that it's a sin. Let her hide it!

The candle in the bottleneck has burned to its end. The night has passed. One already hears the first sounds of the morning, even before one sees the sun. Somewhere someone is opening creaking doors, thumping footsteps can be heard on the stairs, the sky is pale gray, and from the earth a yellowish haze rises, dust and sulfur from the sewers.

Deborah awakes, sighs and says: "It's going to rain! The sewer stinks, close the windows!"

Thus begin the summer days. In the afternoon Mendel can't sleep at home. He goes to the children's playground. He takes pleasure in the song of the rare blackbirds, sits for a long time on a bench, draws jumbled lines in the sand with his umbrella. The sound of the water sprayed by a long rubber hose over the small lawn cools Mendel Singer's face, he believes he feels the water, and he falls asleep. He dreams of the theater, of acrobats in red and gold, of the White House, of the President of the United States, of the billionaire Vanderbilt and of Menuchim.

One day Mac comes. He says (Miriam accompanies him and translates) that he's going to Russia at the end of July or in August to fetch Menuchim.

Mendel suspects why Mac wants to go. He would probably like to marry Miriam. He's doing everything he can for the Singer family.

If I died, thinks Mendel, Mac would marry Miriam. Both of them are waiting for my death. I have time. I'm waiting for Menuchim.

It's June, a hot and especially long month. When will July finally come?

At the end of July Mac orders a ship ticket. They write to the Billes family. Mendel goes to the Skovronneks' shop to tell his friends that his youngest son is coming to America too.

In the Skovronnek family's shop, many more people are gathered than usual. Everyone has a newspaper in his hand. In Europe war has broken out.

Mac will no longer be able to go to Russia. Menuchim will not come to America. War has broken out.

Hadn't the worries just left Mendel Singer? They left, and war broke out.

Jonas was in the war and Menuchim in Russia.

Twice a week, in the evening, Sam and Miriam, Vega and Mac

came to visit Mendel Singer. And they sought to hide from the old man Jonas's certain death and Menuchim's endangered life. It was as if they believed they could divert Mendel's gaze, directed at Europe, onto their own successful achievement and their own security. They placed themselves, so to speak, between Mendel Singer and the war. And while he seemed to listen to their talk, agreed with their speculations that Jonas was employed in an office and Menuchim safe in a Petersburg hospital due to his special illness, he saw his son Jonas fall from his horse and get caught in some of that barbed wire that was so vividly described by the war correspondents. And his little house in Zuchnow was burning – Menuchim lay in the corner and was consumed by flames. Occasionally he ventured to say a short sentence: "A year ago, when the letter came," said Mendel, "I should have gone to Menuchim myself."

No one knew what to reply to that. A few times already Mendel had said that sentence, and always the same silence had ensued. It was as if the old man, with that one sentence, had extinguished the light in the room, it grew dark, and no one could see where to point a finger. And after they had been silent for a long time, they rose and left.

Mendel Singer, however, closed the door behind them, sent Deborah to sleep, lit a candle and began to sing one psalm after another. In good hours he sang them and in bad. He sang them when he thanked heaven and when he feared it. Mendel's swaying movements were always the same. And only by his voice might an attentive listener have recognized whether Mendel, the righteous, was thankful or filled with anxieties. On those nights fear shook him as the wind a weak tree. And worry lent him its voice, with a strange voice he sang the psalms. He was finished. He closed the book, lifted it to his lips, kissed it and snuffed out the flame. But he didn't grow calm. Too little, too little – he said to himself – I have done. Sometimes he was frightened by the realization that his only means, the singing of the psalms, could be powerless in the great storm in which Jonas and Menuchim were going down. The cannons, he thought, are loud, the flames are mighty, my children are burning, it's my fault, my fault! And I sing psalms. It's not enough! It's not enough!

XII

All the people who had wagered, on Skovronnek's political afternoons, that America would remain neutral lost the bet.

It was autumn. At seven in the morning Mendel Singer awoke. At eight he already stood in the street outside the house. The snow was still white and hard, as at home, in Zuchnow. But here it would melt soon. In America it didn't last longer than one night. In the early morning the nimble feet of the newsboys already kneaded it. Mendel Singer waited until one of them passed. He bought a newspaper and went back in the house. The blue petroleum lamp was burning. It illuminated the morning, which was as dark as the night. Mendel Singer unfolded the newspaper, it was greasy, sticky and wet, it smelled like the lamp. He read the reports from the front twice, three times, four times. He noted that fifteen thousand Germans had been taken prisoner at once and that the Russians had resumed their offensive in Bukovina.

That alone did not satisfy him. He took off his glasses, cleaned them, put them back on and read the war reports again. His eyes sifted the lines. Wouldn't the names Sam Singer, Menuchim, Jonas fall out of them? "What's new in the paper?" asked Deborah, as she did every morning. "Nothing at all!" replied Mendel. "The Russians are winning and the Germans are being taken prisoner." It grew quiet. On the spirit stove the tea was boiling. It sang almost like the samovar at home. Only the tea tasted different, it was rancid, American tea, even though the little packages were wrapped in Chinese paper. "You can't even drink tea!" said Mendel, and was surprised himself that he was speaking of such trivialities. Perhaps he wanted to say something else? There were so many important things in the world, and Mendel was complaining about the tea. The Russians were winning, and the Germans were being taken prisoner. Only from Sam one heard nothing at all, and nothing from Menuchim. Two weeks before Mendel had written. And the Red Cross had informed them that Jonas was missing. He's probably dead, Deborah thought inwardly. Mendel thought the same. But they spoke for a long time about the meaning of the word "missing," and as if it completely ruled out the possibility of death, they agreed again and again that "missing" could only mean taken prisoner, deserted or wounded in captivity.

But why hadn't Sam written for so long? Well, he was in the midst of a long march, or currently in a "redeployment," in one of those redeployments the nature and significance of which were more precisely explained in the afternoon at Skovronnek's.

One can't say it aloud, thought Mendel, Sam should not have gone.

Nonetheless, he said the second part of the sentence aloud, Deborah heard it. "You don't understand, Mendel," said Deborah. All the arguments for Sam's participation in the American war Deborah had gotten from her daughter Miriam. "America isn't Russia. America is a fatherland. Every respectable person is duty-bound to go to war for the fatherland. Mac went, Sam couldn't have stayed. Besides, thank God!, he is on the regimental staff. They don't fall there. Because if they permitted all the high officers to fall, they'd never win. And Sam, thank God!, is with the high officers."

"I've given one son to the Tsar, it would have been enough!"

"The Tsar is different, and America is different!"

Mendel didn't debate further. He'd already heard it all. He still remembered the day when they'd departed, Mac and Sam. Both had sung an American song, in the middle of the street. In the evening at Skovronnek's they'd said: Sam was, knock on wood, a good-looking soldier.

Perhaps America was a fatherland, war a duty, cowardice a

disgrace, death impossible on the regimental staff! Nonetheless, thought Mendel, I'm the father, I should have said a word. "Stay, Sam!" I should have said. "I've waited long years to see a tiny sliver of good luck. Now Jonas is in the army, who knows what will happen to Menuchim, you have a wife, a child and a business. Stay, Sam!" Perhaps he would have stayed.

Mendel stood, as was his wont, at the window, his back turned to the room. He looked straight at the Lemmels' broken window, boarded up with brown cardboard, across the street on the second floor. Below was the Jewish butcher shop with the Hebrew sign, white dirty letters on a pale blue background. The Lemmels' son too had gone to war. The whole Lemmel family attended night school and learned English. In the evening they went to school with notebooks, like small children. Probably it was right. Perhaps Mendel and Deborah should go to school too. America was a fatherland.

It was still snowing a little, slow, lazy and damp flakes. The Jews, open black umbrellas rocking over their heads, already began to promenade up and down. More and more came, they walked in the middle of the street, the last white remains of the snow melted under their feet, it was as if they had to walk up and down here at the behest of the authorities until the snow was completely obliterated. Mendel couldn't see the sky from his window. But he knew that it was a dark sky. In all the windows across the street he saw the yellowish red reflection of lamps. Dark was the sky. Dark were all the rooms.

Soon a window was opened here and there, the busts of the neighbor women became visible, they hung red and white bedding and naked, yellowish, skinned pillows from the windows. All of a sudden the whole street was cheerful and colorful. The neighbor women called loud greetings to one another. From inside the rooms sounded the rattle of dishes and the shouts of children. One might have believed it was peacetime, if the war marches hadn't been clanging through the street from the gramophones in the Skovronneks' shop. When is Sunday? thought Mendel. Once he had lived from one Saturday to the next, now he lived from one Sunday to the next. On Sunday Miriam, Vega and his grandson came to visit. They brought letters from Sam or at least news of a general nature. They knew everything, they read all the newspapers. Together they now ran the business. It was always going well, they were industrious, they collected money and waited for Sam's return.

Miriam sometimes brought Mr. Glück, the general manager, with her. She went dancing with Glück, she went swimming with Glück. A new Cossack! thought Mendel. But he said nothing.

"I can't go to the war, unfortunately!" sighed Mr. Glück. "I have a serious heart valve defect, the only thing I inherited from my blessed father." Mendel observed Glück's rosy cheeks, his small brown eyes and his coquettish downy mustache, which he wore against the fashion and with which he often played. He sat between Miriam and Vega. Once, when Mendel stood up from the table in the middle of a conversation, he thought he noticed that Mr. Glück had his right hand in Vega's lap and his left on Miriam's thigh. Mendel went out into the street, he walked up and down outside the house and waited until the guests had gone away. "You're behaving like a Russian Jew," said Deborah, when he returned.

"I am a Russian Jew," replied Mendel. One day, it was a week-day in early February, while Mendel and Deborah were having lunch, Miriam entered.

"Good day, Mother!" she said, "Good day, Father!" and remained standing. Deborah put down her spoon and pushed her plate away. Mendel looked at both women. He knew that something extraordinary had happened. Miriam came on a weekday, at a time when she should have been in the store. His heart beat loudly. But he was calm. He believed he could remember this scene. It had already occurred once before. There stood Miriam in a black raincoat, and was silent. There sat Deborah, she had pushed the plate far away from her, it's almost in the middle of the table, outside it's snowing, soft, lazy and flaky. The lamp burns yellow, its light is greasy, as is its smell. It fights against the dark day, which is weak and dull, but powerful enough to paint the whole room with its pale gray. This light Mendel Singer remembers clearly. He has dreamed this scene. He also knows what's coming. Mendel already knows everything as if it had happened long ago and as if the pain had already years ago turned into grief. Mendel is completely calm.

It's silent for a few seconds. Miriam doesn't speak, as if she hoped that her father or mother would free her, through a question, from the duty to deliver the message. She stands silently. None of the three moves. Mendel stands up and says: "A misfortune has occurred!"

Miriam says: "Mac has come back. He has brought Sam's watch and his last greetings."

Deborah sits, as if nothing had happened, calmly on the armchair. Her eyes are dry and empty, like two dark little pieces of glass. She sits opposite the window and it looks as if she were counting the snowflakes.

It's quiet, one hears the hard ticking of the clock. Suddenly Deborah begins, very slowly, with creeping fingers, to tear out her hair. She pulls one plait of hair after another over her face, which is pale and motionless, like swollen plaster. Then she tears out one strand after another, almost in the same tempo in which the snowflakes are falling outside. Already two or three white islands appear in the middle of her hair, a few coin-sized spots of naked scalp and very tiny drops of red blood. No one moves. The clock ticks, the snow falls, and Deborah gently tears out her hair.

Miriam sinks to her knees, buries her head in Deborah's lap and stops moving. In Deborah's face not a feature changes. Her two hands take turns pulling at her hair. Her hands look like pale, fleshy five-footed animals that feed on hair.

Mendel stands, his arms folded over the back of the armchair.

Deborah begins to sing. She sings with a deep, manly voice that sounds as if an invisible singer were in the room. The strange voice sings an old Jewish song without words, a black lullaby for dead children.

Miriam rises, straightens her hat, goes to the door and lets Mac in.

He is larger in uniform than in civilian clothing. In both hands, which he holds in front of him like plates, he has Sam's watch, wallet and coin purse.

These objects Mac lays slowly on the table, directly before Deborah. He watches her tearing out her hair for a while, then he goes to Mendel, lays his large hands on the old man's shoulders and weeps soundlessly. His tears stream, a heavy rain over his uniform. It's quiet, Deborah's song has ceased, the clock ticks, the evening sinks suddenly over the world, the lamp no longer glows yellow but white, behind the windowpanes the world is black, one can see no more flakes. All of a sudden a wailing sound comes out of Deborah's breast. It sounds like the rest of that melody she was singing before, a ruptured, shattered note.

Then Deborah falls from the armchair. She lies, a contorted soft mass, on the floor.

Mac flings open the door, leaves it open, it grows cold in the room.

He comes back, a doctor accompanies him, a small nimble gray-haired man.

Miriam stands opposite her father.

Mac and the doctor carry Deborah to the bed.

The doctor sits on the edge of the bed and says: "She is dead."

Menuchim too is dead, alone, among strangers, thinks Mendel Singer.

XIII

Seven round days Mendel Singer sat on a stool next to the wardrobe and looked at the windowpane, on which a white scrap of canvas hung as a sign of mourning and in which day and night one of the two blue lamps burned. Seven round days rolled away in succession like large black slow wheels, without beginning and without end, round like grief. One after another came the neighbors: Menkes, Skovronnek, Rottenberg and Groschel, brought hard-boiled eggs and bagels for Mendel Singer, round foods, without beginning and without end, round like the seven days of mourning. Mendel spoke little with his visitors. He scarcely noticed that they came and went. Day and night his door stood open with the unlocked, pointless bolt. Whoever wanted to come came, whoever wanted to leave left. This visitor and that tried to begin a conversation. But Mendel Singer avoided it. He talked, while the others spoke of living things, with his dead wife. "You have it good, Deborah!" he said to her. "It's only a shame that you left behind no son, I myself have to say the prayer for the dead, but I will soon die, and no one will weep for us. Like two little specks of dust we were blown away. Like two little sparks we are extinguished. I've begotten children, your womb has borne them, death has taken them. Full of need and without meaning was your life. In young years I enjoyed your flesh, in later years I spurned it. Perhaps that was our sin. Because the warmth of love was not in us, but between us the frost of habit, everything around us died, everything wasted away and was ruined. You have it good, Deborah. The Lord has taken pity on you. You're dead and buried. For me He has no pity. For I'm a dead man and live. He is the Lord, He knows what He is doing. If you can, pray for me, that I may be effaced from the book of the living.

See, Deborah, the neighbors come to me, to console me. But though they are many and they all strain their heads, they nonetheless find no consolation for my situation. Still my heart beats, still my eyes see, still my limbs move, still my feet walk. I eat and drink, pray and breathe. But my blood freezes, my hands are limp, my heart is empty. I am no longer Mendel Singer, I am the remains of Mendel Singer. America has killed us. America is a fatherland, but a deadly fatherland. What was day at home is here night. What was life at home is here death. The son who at home was named Shemariah was here named Sam. In America you are buried, Deborah, I too, Mendel Singer, will be buried in America."

On the morning of the eighth day, when Mendel stood up from his grieving, his daughter-in-law Vega came, accompanied by Mr.

Glück. "Mr. Singer," said Mr. Glück, "the car is waiting below. You must come with us immediately, something has happened to Miriam." "All right," replied Mendel indifferently, as if someone had informed him that his room had to be wallpapered. "All right, give me my coat."

Mendel crept into the coat with weak arms and went down the stairs. Mr. Glück rushed him into the car. They drove and didn't speak a word. Mendel didn't ask what had happened to Miriam. Probably she is dead too, he thought calmly. Mac has killed her out of jealousy.

For the first time he entered the apartment of his dead son. He was pushed into a room. There lay Miriam, in a broad white bed. Her hair flowed loosely, in a sparkling blue-black, over the white pillows. Her face glowed red, and her black eyes had wide round red outlines; circled by rings of fire were Miriam's eyes. A nurse sat next to her, Mac stood in a corner, large and motionless, like a piece of furniture.

"There is Mendel Singer," cried Miriam. She stretched out a hand toward her father and began to laugh. Her laughter lasted a few minutes. It sounded like the ringing of the high-pitched incessant signals at train stations and as if someone were striking with a thousand brass mallets against a thousand thin crystal glasses. Suddenly the laughter broke off. For a second it was silent. Then Miriam began to sob. She threw off the blanket, her naked legs writhed, her feet kicked with a swift steady rhythm on the white bed, ever swifter and steadier, while her balled fists swung in the same rhythm through the air. The nurse held Miriam down with force. She grew calmer.

"Good day, Mendel Singer!" said Miriam. "You are my father, I can tell you. I love Mac, who is standing over there, but I've deceived him. I've slept with Mr. Glück, yes, with Mr. Glück! Glück is my Glück, Mac is my Mac. I like Mendel Singer too, and if you want – " Here the nurse held her hand over Miriam's mouth, and Miriam fell silent. Mendel Singer was still standing at the door, Mac was still standing in the corner. Both men stared intently at each other. Because they couldn't communicate with words, they spoke with their eyes. "She is mad," said Mendel Singer's eyes to those of Mac. "She couldn't live without men, she is mad."

Vega entered and said: "We've called the doctor. Any moment now he should be here. Since yesterday Miriam's been speaking incoherently. She went for a walk with Mac, and when they returned she began to behave in this incomprehensible way. Any moment now the doctor should be here."

The doctor arrived. He was a German, he could communicate with Mendel. "We will bring her to the asylum," said the doctor. "Your daughter, I'm afraid, has to go to an asylum. Wait a moment, I will anesthetize her."

Mac was still standing in the room. "Will you hold her down?" asked the doctor. Mac held Miriam down with his large hands. The doctor pushed a syringe into her thigh. "Soon she will be calm," he said.

The ambulance came, two carriers entered the room with a

stretcher. Miriam was asleep. They bound her to the stretcher. Mendel, Mac and Vega drove behind the ambulance.

"You didn't live to see this," Mendel spoke to his wife Deborah as they drove. "I'm still living through it, but I've known it all along. Ever since that evening when I saw Miriam with the Cossack in the field, I've known it. The devil has entered her. Pray for us, Deborah, that he leaves her again."

Now Mendel sat in the waiting room of the asylum, surrounded by others waiting in front of small tables, on which vases full of yellow summer flowers stood, and thin racks laden with illustrated magazines. But none of the people waiting smelled the flowers, none of them leafed through the magazines. At first Mendel believed that all the people sitting here with him were mad and he himself a lunatic like the rest. Then he saw through the broad door of shining glass, which separated the waiting room from the whitewashed corridor, people in blue-striped gowns being led past in pairs. First women, then men, and occasionally one of the patients cast a wild, pinched, deranged, evil face through the pane of the door into the waiting room. All the people waiting shivered, only Mendel remained calm. Yes, it seemed strange to him that the people waiting weren't wearing blue-striped gowns too and that he himself wasn't. He sat in a broad leather armchair, the cap of black silk rep he had put over his knee, his umbrella leaned, a faithful companion, next to the chair. Mendel glanced alternately at the people, the glass door, the magazines, the lunatics, who were still passing by outside – they were being led to the bath – and the golden flowers in the vases. They were yellow cowslips, Mendel remembered that he had often seen them at home on the green meadows. The flowers came from his homeland. He recalled them happily. Those meadows had been there, and those flowers! Peace had been at home there, youth had been at home there, and familiar poverty. In summer the sky had been very blue, the sun very hot, the grain very yellow, the flies had glistened green and hummed warm little songs, and high below the blue sky the larks had trilled, without cease. Mendel Singer forgot, as he looked at the cowslips, that Deborah was dead, Sam fallen, Miriam mad and Jonas missing. It was as if he had only just now lost his homeland and in it Menuchim, the most faithful of all the dead, the farthest away of all the dead, the closest of all the dead. If we had stayed there – thought Mendel – nothing at all would have happened! Jonas was right, Jonas, the dumbest of my children! He loved horses, he loved schnapps, he loved girls, now he is missing! Jonas, I will never see you again, I won't be able to tell you that you were right to become a Cossack. "Why do you people always roam around in the world?" Sameshkin had said. "The devil sends you!" He was a peasant, Sameshkin, a shrewd peasant. Mendel hadn't wanted to go. Deborah, Miriam, Shemariah – they had wanted to go, to wander around in the world. They should have stayed, loved horses, drunk schnapps, slept in the meadows, let Miriam run around with Cossacks and loved Menuchim.

Have I gone mad, Mendel thought, that I'm thinking this way? Does an old Jew think such things? God has confused my thoughts, the devil is thinking in me, as he is speaking from my daughter Miriam.

The doctor came, drew Mendel into a corner and said softly: "Brace yourself, your daughter is very ill. There are many such cases these days, the war, you understand, and the misfortune in the world, it's a bad time. The medical field doesn't yet know how to cure this illness. One of your sons is an epileptic, I hear, I'm sorry to say that something like that runs in the family. We doctors call it degenerative psychosis. It can pass. But it can also turn out to be an illness that we doctors call dementia, dementia praecox, but even the names are uncertain. It is one of the rare cases that we can't cure. But you are a pious man, Mr. Singer? God can help. Just pray diligently to the good Lord. By the way, do you want to see your daughter once more? Come with me!"

A bunch of keys rattled, a door slammed loudly, and Mendel walked through a long corridor past white doors with black numbers, like upright coffins. Again the attendant's keys rattled, and one of the coffins was opened, inside lay Miriam, asleep, Mac and Vega stood beside her.

"Now we have to go," said the doctor.

"Take me directly home, to my street," commanded Mendel.

His voice sounded so hard that all were startled. They looked at him. His appearance didn't seem to have changed. And yet it was another Mendel. He was dressed exactly as he had been in Zuchnow and the whole time in America. In high boots, in a half-long caftan, with the cap of black silk rep. What had changed him so?

Why did he appear taller and statelier to them all? Why did such a white and terrible glow emanate from his face? He almost seemed to tower above the tall Mac. His Majesty, pain, thought the doctor, has entered the old Jew.

"Once," began Mendel in the car, "Sam said to me that American medicine is the best in the world. Now it can't help. God can help! says the doctor. Tell me, Vega, have you ever seen God help a Mendel Singer? God can help!"

"You will live with us," said Vega with a sob. "I will not live with you, my child," answered Mendel, "you will take a husband, you shouldn't be without a husband, your child shouldn't be without a father. I'm an old Jew, Vega, soon I will die. Listen, Vega! Mac was Shemariah's friend, he loved Miriam, I know, he is not a Jew, but you should marry him, not Mr. Glück! Do you hear, Vega? Does it surprise you that I'm talking like this, Vega? Don't be surprised, I'm not mad. I've gotten old, I've seen a few worlds perish, finally I've grown wise. All those years I was a foolish teacher. Now I know what I'm saying."

They arrived, they unloaded Mendel, led him into his room, Mac and Vega stood for a while and didn't know what to do.

Mendel sat down on the stool next to the wardrobe and said to Vega, "Don't forget what I told you. Now go, my children." They left him. Mendel went to the window and watched them climb into the car. It seemed to him that he should bless them, as one blesses children who are starting on a very hard or a very happy path. I will never see them again, he thought, and I won't bless them. My blessing would only become a curse for them, their encounter with me a detriment. He felt light, yes, lighter than ever in all his years. He had severed all relationships. It occurred to him that he had already been alone for years. He had been alone since the moment desire had ceased between his wife and him. Alone, he was alone. Wife and children had surrounded him and had prevented him from bearing his pain. Like useless bandages that don't help one heal, they had lain on his wounds and had only covered them. Now, finally, he savored his woe with triumph. There was only one relationship left to break. He set to work.

He went into the kitchen, gathered up newspaper and pine chips and made a fire in the open stove. When the fire reached a considerable height and width, Mendel walked with strong strides to the wardrobe and took from it the little red velvet sack that contained his phylacteries, his prayer shawl and his prayer books. He imagined how these objects would burn. The flames will seize the yellow-toned shawl of pure sheep's wool and destroy it with pointed bluish greedy tongues. The glittering edge of silver threads will slowly become charred, in small red-hot spirals. The fire will gently curl up the pages of the books, turn them into silver-gray ashes, and for a few moments dye the black letters bloody. The leather corners of the bindings unfurl, stand up like strange ears with which the books listen to what Mendel calls after them into the hot death. He calls a terrible song after them. "It's over, over, over for Mendel Singer," he cries, and with his boots he stamps in time to it, so that the floorboards boom and the pots on the wall begin to rattle. "He has no son, he has no daughter, he has no wife, he has no homeland, he has no money. God says: I have punished Mendel Singer. Why does He punish him? Why not Lemmel, the butcher? Why doesn't He punish Skovronnek? Why doesn't He punish Menkes? Only Mendel He punishes! Mendel has death, Mendel has madness, Mendel has hunger, all the gifts of God Mendel has. It's over, over, over for Mendel Singer."

Thus Mendel stood before the open fire and shouted and stamped with his feet. He held the little red velvet sack, but he did not throw it in. A few times he lifted it up in the air, but his arms lowered it again. His heart was angry with God, but in his muscles the fear of God still dwelled. Fifty years, day after day, these hands had spread the prayer shawl and folded it again, unrolled the phylacteries and wrapped them around the head and around the left arm, opened this prayer book, turned the pages over and over and closed it again. Now Mendel's hands refused to obey his rage. Only his mouth, which had so often prayed, did not refuse. Only his feet, which had often jumped with a hallelujah to the glory of God, stamped in time to Mendel's song of rage.

Because Mendel's neighbors heard screaming and banging, and because they saw the gray-blue smoke penetrating through the cracks and gaps of his door into the stairwell, they knocked on Singer's door and shouted to him to open for them. But he didn't hear them. His eyes were filled with the smoke of the fire, and in his ears roared his great painful jubilation. The neighbors were already prepared to fetch the police when one of them said: "Let's call his friends! They're sitting at Skovronnek's. Maybe they can bring the poor man back to his senses."

When his friends arrived, Mendel actually did calm down. He unbolted the door and let them in, one after another, as they had always been accustomed to enter Mendel's room, Menkes, Skovronnek, Rottenberg and Groschel. They compelled Mendel to sit down on the bed, themselves sat down next to and in front of him, and Menkes said: "What's the matter, Mendel? Why are you making a fire, why do you want to set the house on fire?"

"I want to burn more than just a house and more than a person. You will be astonished when I tell you what I really intended to burn. You will be astonished and say: Mendel is mad too, like his daughter. But I assure you: I am not mad. I was mad. For more than sixty years I was mad, today I am not."

"So tell us what you want to burn!"

"I want to burn God."

A cry escaped from all four listeners at the same time. They weren't all pious and God-fearing, as Mendel had always been. All four had lived long enough in America, they worked on the Sabbath, their interest was in money, and the dust of the world already lay thick, high and gray on their ancient faith. Many customs they had forgotten, numerous laws they had violated, with their heads and limbs they had sinned. But God still dwelled in their hearts. And when Mendel blasphemed God, they felt as if he had grasped their naked hearts with sharp fingers.

"Do not blaspheme, Mendel," Skovronnek said after a long

silence. "You know better than I, because you have studied much more, that God's blows have a hidden meaning. We don't know why we are punished."

"But I know, Skovronnek," replied Mendel. "God is cruel, and the more one obeys Him, the more severely He deals with us. He is mightier than the mighty, with the nail of His little finger He can wipe them out, but He doesn't do it. Only the weak he gladly destroys. The weakness of a man provokes His strength, and obedience arouses His wrath. He is a great cruel *ispravnik*. If you follow the laws, He says you have followed them only for your own advantage. And if you violate just one commandment, He persecutes you with a hundred punishments. If you try to bribe Him, He puts you on trial. And if you deal honestly with Him, He lies in wait for the bribe. In all of Russia there is no worse *ispravnik*!"

"Remember, Mendel," began Rottenberg, "remember Job. The same sort of things happened to him as to you. He sat on the naked earth, ashes on his head, and his wounds hurt him so much that he writhed on the ground like an animal. He too blasphemed God. And yet it had only been a test. What do we know, Mendel, of what is going on up above? Maybe the evil one came before God and said as he did then: We must tempt a righteous one. And the Lord said: Just try it with Mendel, my servant."

"And there you also see," Groschel chimed in, "that your reproach is unjust. For Job wasn't weak when God began to test him, but powerful. And you weren't weak either, Mendel! Your son had a store, a department store, he got richer from year to year. Your son Menuchim almost recovered, and he almost came to America too. You were healthy, your wife was healthy, your daughter was beautiful, and soon you would have found a husband for her!"

"Why do you break my heart, Groschel?" replied Mendel. "Why do you enumerate for me all that was, now that nothing remains? My wounds aren't yet healed, and already you tear them open."

"He is right," said the other three, as if with one mouth.

And Rottenberg began: "Your heart is broken, Mendel, I know that. But because we can talk about anything with you and because you know that we bear your pains as if we were your brothers, will you be angry with us if I ask you to think of Menuchim? Maybe, dear Mendel, you tried to disturb God's plans, because you left Menuchim behind? A sick son was granted to you, and you acted as if he were an evil son." It was silent. For a long time Mendel answered nothing at all. When he began to talk again, it was as if he hadn't heard Rottenberg's words; for he turned to Groschel and said:

"And what do you want with the example of Job? Have you ever seen real miracles, with your eyes? Miracles as they are reported at the end of Job? Shall my son Shemariah be resurrected from the mass grave in France? Shall my son Jonas come to life from his disappearance? Shall my daughter Miriam suddenly return home healthy from the insane asylum? And if she returns home, will she still find a husband there and be able to live on peacefully like someone who has never been mad? Shall my wife Deborah rise from the grave while it's still damp? Shall my son Menuchim, in the middle of the war, come here from Russia, supposing that he's still alive? For it is not correct," and here Mendel turned back to Rottenberg, "that I left Menuchim behind maliciously and so as to punish him. For other reasons, because of my daughter, who had begun to run around with Cossacks – with Cossacks! – we had to leave. And why was Menuchim sick? His illness was already a sign that God is angry with me – and the first of the blows that I did not deserve."

"Even though God can do anything," began the most thoughtful of them all, Menkes, "it is nonetheless probable that He no longer performs the truly great miracles, because the world is no longer worthy of them. And even if God wanted to make an exception for you, the sins of the others would still stand in His way. For the others aren't worthy of seeing a miracle befall a righteous man, and that is why Lot had to emigrate and Sodom and Gomorrah were destroyed and did not see the miracle bestowed on Lot. But today the world is inhabited everywhere – and even if you emigrate, the newspapers will report what happened to you. So these days God must only perform moderate miracles. But they are big enough, praised be His name! Your wife Deborah cannot come to life, your son Shemariah cannot come to life. But Menuchim is probably alive, and after the war you can see him. Your son Jonas might be in war captivity, and after the war you can see him. Your daughter can recover, the confusion will be taken from her, she can be more beautiful than ever, and she will get a husband, and she will bear grandchildren for you. And you have a grandson, Shemariah's son. Gather together your love, which you had until now for all your children, for this one grandson! And you will be consoled."

"Between me and my grandson," replied Mendel, "the bond has been broken, because Shemariah is dead, my son and the father of my grandson. My daughter-in-law Vega will marry another man, my grandson will have a new father, whose father I am not. The house of my son is not my house. I have no place there. My presence brings misfortune, and my love draws down the curse as a lone tree in a flat field the lightning. But as for Miriam, the doctor himself told me that medicine could not cure her illness. Jonas is probably dead, and Menuchim was sick, even if he was doing better. In the middle of Russia, in such a dangerous war, he will certainly have perished. No, my friends! I am alone and I want to be alone. All these years I have loved God, and He has hated me. All these years I have feared Him, now He can do nothing more to me. All the arrows from His quiver have already struck me. All He can do now is kill me. But for that He is too cruel. I will live, live, live."

"But His power," Groschel objected, "is in this world and in the next. Woe to you, Mendel, when you are dead!"

Then Mendel laughed heartily and said: "I am not afraid of hell, my skin is already burned, my limbs are already lamed, and the evil spirits are my friends. All the torments of hell I have already suffered. The devil is kinder than God. Because he is not as powerful, he cannot be as cruel. I am not afraid, my friends!"

At that his friends fell silent. But they didn't want to leave Mendel alone, and so they remained sitting silently. Groschel, the youngest, went down to inform the others' wives and his own that the men would not come home that evening. He brought another five Jews to Mendel Singer's apartment so that they would be ten and could say the evening prayer. They began to pray. But Mendel Singer did not participate in the prayer. He sat on the bed and didn't move. Even the prayer for the dead he did not say – and Menkes said it for him. The five strangers left the house. But the four friends stayed all night. One of the two blue lamps was still burning with the last remains of the wick and the last drop of oil on the flat bottom. It was silent. This man and that fell asleep in his seat, snored and awoke, disturbed by his own noises, and nodded off again.

Only Mendel didn't sleep. His eyes wide open, he looked at the window, behind which the dense blackness of the night finally began to thin out, then turned gray, then whitish. Six strokes sounded from inside the clock. Then his friends awoke, one after another. And without their having arranged it, they grasped Mendel by the arms and led him downstairs. They brought him into the Skovronnek's back room and laid him on a sofa.

Here he fell asleep.

XIV

From that morning on Mendel Singer stayed with the Skovron-neks. His friends sold his scanty furniture. They left only the bedding behind and the red velvet sack with the prayer utensils, which Mendel had almost burned. The sack Mendel no longer touched. In the Skovronneks' back room it hung gray and dusty on a mighty nail. Mendel Singer no longer prayed. True, he was sometimes used when a tenth man was missing, to complete the prescribed number of worshippers. Then he let his presence be counted. Occasionally he also lent this man and that his phylacteries for a small fee. It was rumored that he often went over to the Italian quarter to eat pork and anger God. The people in whose midst he lived took Mendel's side in the battle he was waging against heaven. Even though they were devout, they had to concede that the Jew was right. Jehovah had dealt with him too harshly.

Still war was in the world. Apart from Sam, Mendel's son, all the residents of the neighborhood who had gone into the field were alive. Young Lemmel had become an officer and had been lucky enough to lose his left hand. He came on furlough and was the hero of the neighborhood. He granted all the Jews the right to a homeland in America. He only remained on the base to put the finishing touches on fresh troops. As great as the difference between young Lemmel and old Singer was, the Jews of the neighborhood placed the two of them in a certain proximity. It was as if the Jews believed that Mendel and Lemmel had divided between themselves the sum total of misfortune intended for all. And Mendel had lost more than just a left hand! If Lemmel fought against the Germans, Mendel fought against heavenly powers. And even though they were convinced that the old man was no longer in full possession of his faculties, the Jews nonetheless could not help mingling admiration with their sympathy, and reverence before the holiness of madness. Without doubt, Mendel Singer was elected. As a pitiful witness to the cruel power of Jehovah he lived in the midst of the others, whose laborious weekdays no terror disturbed. For long years he had lived his days as they all did, observed by few, not noticed at all by some. One day he was distinguished in a dreadful way. There was no one left who did not know him. He spent most of the day in the street. It was as if it were part of his curse not only to suffer misfortune without precedent but also to bear the sign of sorrow like a banner. And like a guard of his own agonies he walked up and down in the middle of the street, greeted by all, given small coins by some, spoken to by many. For the alms he did not give thanks, the greetings he rarely returned and questions he answered with yes or no. Early in the morning he rose. No light entered the Skovronneks' back room, it had no window. He only felt the morning through the shutters, the morning had a long way to go before it reached Mendel Singer. When the first sounds stirred in the streets, Singer began the day. On the spirit stove the tea boiled. He drank it with bread and a hard-boiled egg. He cast a shy but angry glance at the sack with the holy objects on the wall, in the dark blue shadow the little sack looked like a still darker outgrowth of the shadow. "I don't pray!" Mendel said to himself. But it hurt him that he didn't pray. His rage pained him, and the powerlessness of that rage. Even though Mendel was angry with God, God still ruled over the world. Hate could grasp him no more than piety.

Filled with such reflections and others like them, Mendel began his day. Once, he remembered, his awakening had been easy, the joyful anticipation of the prayer had roused him and the desire to renew his conscious closeness to God. From the cozy warmth of sleep he had entered the still more homelike, still more intimate glow of prayer, as if it were a splendid and nonetheless familiar hall, in which the mighty and yet smiling father dwelled. "Good morning, Father!" Mendel Singer had said – and believed that he heard an answer. It had been a deception. The hall was splendid and cold, the father was mighty and angry. No sound passed his lips but thunder.

Mendel Singer unlocked the shop, put the sheet music, the song lyrics, the gramophone records in the narrow display window and pulled up the iron shutters with a long rod. Then he took a mouthful of water, sprinkled the floor, grabbed the broom and swept up the dirt of the previous day. On a small dustpan he carried the scraps of paper to the stove and made a fire and burned them. Then he went out, bought a few newspapers and brought them to some neighbors' houses. He met the milk boy and the early bakers, greeted them and went back "to business." Soon the

Skovronneks came. They sent him on this errand and that. All day it was: "Mendel, run out and buy a herring," "Mendel, the raisins haven't been soaked yet!" "Mendel, you've forgotten the laundry!" "Mendel, the ladder is broken!" "A pane is missing in the lantern," "Where is the corkscrew?" And Mendel ran out and bought a herring and soaked the raisins and fetched the laundry and repaired the ladder and carried the lantern to the glazier and found the corkscrew. The neighbors sometimes asked him to watch the small children when a movie house had changed its program or a new theater had come. And Mendel sat among the strange children, and as he had once rocked Menuchim's basket at home with a light and tender finger, now he rocked, with the light and tender tips of his toes, the cradles of strange infants whose names he did not know. Meanwhile he sang an old song, a very old song: "Say after me, Menuchim: 'In the beginning God created the heaven and the earth,' say it after me, Menuchim!"

It was in the month of Elul, and the high holy days were beginning. All the Jews of the neighborhood wanted to set up a temporary temple in Skovronnek's back room. (For they did not like to go to the synagogue.) "Mendel, we will pray in your room!" said Skovronnek. "What do you say to that?" "Go ahead and pray!" replied Mendel. And he watched as the Jews gathered, lit the great yellow wax candles with the overhanging wick clusters. He himself helped every merchant roll down the shutters and lock the doors. He saw how they all put on the white robes, so that they looked like corpses that had risen again to praise God. They took off their shoes and stood in their socks. They fell to their knees and rose, the great golden-yellow wax candles and the snow-white ones of stearin bent and dripped hot tears on the prayer shawls, which encrusted in no time. The white Jews themselves bent like the candles, and their tears too fell on the floor and dried. But Mendel Singer stood black and silent, in his everyday clothing, in the background, near the door, and didn't move. His lips were closed and his heart a stone. The singing of the Kol Nidre arose like a hot wind. Mendel Singer's lips remained closed and his heart a stone. Black and silent, in his everyday clothing, he stayed in the background, near the door. No one paid attention to him. The Jews took pains not to see him. He was a stranger among them. This one and that thought of him and prayed for him. But Mendel Singer stood upright by the door and was angry with God. They are all praying because they are afraid, he thought. But I am not afraid. I am not afraid!

After everyone had left, Mendel Singer lay down on his hard sofa. It was still warm from the bodies of the worshippers. Forty candles were still burning in the room. He did not dare extinguish them, they kept him from falling asleep. Thus he lay awake all night. He thought up unprecedented blasphemies. He imagined going out now, to the Italian quarter, buying pork in a restaurant and returning to consume it here, in the company of the silently burning candles. He even untied his handkerchief and counted his coins, but he didn't leave the room and ate nothing. He lay with his clothes on, with large wakeful eyes, on the sofa and murmured:

"It's over, over, over for Mendel Singer! He has no son, he has no daughter, he has no wife, he has no money, he has no house, he has no God! It's over, over, over for Mendel Singer!" The golden and bluish flames of the candles trembled softly. The hot, wax tears dripped with hard blows on the candlestick bases, on the yellow sand in the brass mortars, on the dark green glass of the bottles. The hot breath of the worshippers was still living in the room. On the temporary chairs that had been set up for them, their white prayer shawls still lay and waited for the morning and for the continuation of the prayer. It smelled of wax and charred wicks. Mendel left the room, opened the shop, stepped outside. It was a clear autumnal night. No one was in sight. Mendel walked up and down in front of the shop. The broad, slow steps of the policeman sounded. Then Mendel went back into the shop. He still avoided men in uniform.

The time of the holidays was over, autumn came, the rain sang. Mendel bought some herring, swept the floor, fetched the laundry, repaired the ladder, looked for the corkscrew, soaked the raisins, walked up and down in the middle of the street. For alms he rarely gave thanks, greetings he didn't return, questions he answered with yes or no. In the afternoon, when people gathered to talk politics and read aloud from the newspapers, Mendel lay down on the sofa and slept. The talk of the others didn't wake him. The war had nothing at all to do with him. The newest records sang him to sleep. He awoke only when it was silent and everyone was gone. Then he spoke for a while with old Skovronnek.

"Your daughter-in-law is getting married," said Skovronnek once.

"Good!" replied Mendel.

"But she is marrying Mac!"

"I advised her to do that!"

"The business is going well!"

"It is not my business."

"Mac has let us know that he wants to give you money!"

"I don't want money!"

"Good night, Mendel!"

"Good night, Skovronnek!"

The terrible news flared up in the newspapers, which Mendel customarily bought each morning. It flared up, he perceived against his will its distant reflection, he wanted to know nothing about it. Russia was no longer ruled by the Tsar. Fine, let the Tsar cease to rule. About Jonas and Menuchim, in any case, they had nothing to report, the newspapers. They bet at Skovronnek's that the war would be over in a month. Fine, let the war end. Shemariah wasn't coming back. The head of the insane asylum wrote that Miriam's condition had not improved. Vega sent the letter, Skovronnek read it to Mendel. "Fine," said Mendel, "Miriam will not recover!"

His old black caftan shimmered green on the shoulders, and like a tiny drawing of the spine the seam became visible down the whole back. The skirts of his coat grew longer and longer and no longer touched, when Mendel walked, the shafts of his boots, but almost his ankles. His beard, which had once covered only his chest, reached down to the last buttons of the caftan. The visor of the cap of black, now greenish, rep had grown soft and pliable and hung limply over Mendel Singer's eyes, not unlike a rag. In his pockets Mendel Singer carried many things: packages people had sent him to pick up, newspapers, various tools with which he repaired the damaged objects at Skovronnek's, balls of colored string, packing paper and bread. These weights bowed Mendel's back still lower, and because the right pocket was usually heavier than the left, it pulled down the old man's right shoulder too. Thus he walked slanted and stooped through the street, a dilapidated man, with buckling knees and shuffling soles. The news of the world and the weekdays and holidays of the others rolled past him, as carriages past an old remote house.

One day the war was really over. The neighborhood was empty. The people had gone to see the peace celebrations and the home-coming of the regiments. Many had asked Mendel to watch their houses. He went from one apartment to another, checked the latches and locks and returned home, to the shop. From an immeasurable distance he believed that he heard the festive roar of the joyful world, the explosion of fireworks and the laughter of tens of thousands of people. A small quiet peace came over him. His fingers stroked his beard, his lips curled into a smile, even a tiny giggle came in brief bursts from his throat. "Mendel will celebrate too," he whispered, and for the first time he approached one of the brown gramophone boxes. He had already seen how one wound up the instrument. "A record, a record!" he said. That morning a returned soldier had been there and had brought half a dozen records, new songs from Europe. Mendel unpacked the top one, laid it carefully on the instrument, reflected for a while, trying to remember exactly how it worked, and finally put the needle on. The apparatus coughed. Then the song sounded. It was evening, Mendel stood in the dark next to the gramophone and listened. Every day he had heard songs here, comical ones and sad ones, slow ones and fast ones, dark ones and light ones. But never had there been a song like this one. It ran like a little stream and murmured gently, grew great as the sea and roared. "I am hearing the whole world now," thought Mendel. How is it possible that the whole world is engraved on such a small disk? As a little silver flute came in and from then on never again left the velvety violin and edged it like a faithful narrow seam, Mendel began for the first time in a long while to weep. Then the song was over. He put it on again and a third time. He sang along, finally, with his hoarse voice and drummed with timid fingers on the box's stand.

Thus Skovronnek, returning, found him. He turned off the gramophone and said: "Mendel, light the lamp! What are you playing here?" Mendel lit the lamp. "See, Skovronnek, what the little song is called." "Those are the new records," said Skovronnek. "I bought them today. The song is called – " and Skovronnek put on his glasses, held the record under the lamp and read: "The song is called: 'Menuchim's Song.'"

Mendel was suddenly weak. He had to sit down. He stared at the shining record in Skovronnek's hands.

"I know what you're thinking," said Skovronnek.

"Yes," answered Mendel.

Skovronnek turned the crank again. "A beautiful song," said Skovronnek, leaned his head on his left shoulder and listened. Gradually the shop filled up with the tardy neighbors. No one spoke. All listened to the song and rocked their heads in time to it.

And they listened to it sixteen times, until they knew it by heart.

Mendel remained alone in the shop. He carefully locked the door from inside, cleared out the display window, began to undress. Each of his steps was accompanied by the song. As he fell asleep, it seemed to him that the blue and silver melody merged with the pitiful whimper, with Menuchim's, his own Menuchim's only, long unheard song.

XV

The days grew longer. The mornings already contained so much brightness that they could even break through the closed iron shutters into Mendel's windowless back room. In April the street awoke a good hour earlier. Mendel lit the spirit stove, put on the tea, filled the small blue washbasin, plunged his face in the bowl, dried himself with the corner of the towel that hung on the door latch, opened the shutters, took a mouthful of water, carefully spat it on the floorboards and gazed at the winding ornaments that the bright spray from his lips drew in the dust. Already the spirit stove hissed; the clock hadn't even struck six yet. Mendel stepped outside. The windows were opening in the street, as if of their own accord. It was spring.

It was spring. People were preparing for Easter,* in all the houses Mendel helped. He planed the wooden tabletops to rid them of the profane remains of food from the whole year. The round, cylindrical packages in which the Easter bread was stacked in crimson paper he placed on the white shelves of the display windows, and the wines from Palestine he freed from the cobwebs under which they had been resting in the cool cellars. He took apart the neighbors' beds and carried them piece by piece into the courtyards, where the mild April sun lured out the vermin and delivered them to extermination with gasoline, turpentine and petroleum. In pink and sky-blue decorative paper he cut with scissors round and angular holes and fringes and attached the paper with thumbtacks to the kitchen racks as an artful covering for the

---

*Perhaps to avoid terms that would be unfamiliar to non-Jewish readers of his time, Roth refers to the Jewish Passover feast, *Pesach*, by the name of the Christian holiday Easter (*Ostern* in German) celebrated at the same time of year and calls *matzoh*, the unleavened bread eaten at Passover, "Easter bread" (*Osterbrot*). [Translator]

dishes. The casks and tubs he filled with hot water, great iron balls he held in the stove fire on wooden rods until they glowed. Then he submerged the balls in the tubs and casks, the water hissed, the vessels were purified, as the rule commanded. In gigantic mortars he pounded the Easter bread into flour, poured it into clean sacks and tied them with blue ribbons. All this he had once done in his own house. Spring had come more slowly there than in America. Mendel remembered the aging gray snow that lined the wooden pavement of the sidewalk in Zuchnow at this time of year, the crystal icicles on the edge of the faucets, the sudden gentle rains that sang in the gutters all night long, the distant thunder that rolled away behind the pine forest, the white frost that tenderly covered each light blue morning, Menuchim, whom Miriam had stuck into a roomy barrel to get him out of the way, and the hope that finally, finally this year the Messiah would come. He didn't come. He isn't coming, thought Mendel, he will not come. Let others wait for him. Mendel wasn't waiting.

Nonetheless, this spring Mendel seemed to his friends and neighbors to have changed. They observed sometimes that he hummed a song, and they caught a gentle smile under his white beard.

"He's becoming childish, he's already old," said Groschel.

"He has forgotten everything," said Rottenberg.

"It's a pleasure before death," declared Menkes.

Skovronnek, who knew him best, was silent. Only once, one evening before going to sleep, he said to his wife, "Ever since the new records came, our Mendel is another man. I catch him sometimes winding up a gramophone himself. What do you think about that?"

"I think," Mrs. Skovronnek replied impatiently, "that Mendel is getting old and childish and will soon be useless." She had already been dissatisfied with Mendel for some time. The older he became, the less sympathy she had for him. Gradually she also forgot that Mendel had been a wealthy man, and her compassion, which had been nourished by her respect (for her heart was small), died away. She also no longer addressed him as she had in the beginning: Mr. Singer – but simply: Mendel, as almost the whole world did. And if she had formerly given him orders with a certain restraint meant to show that his compliance at once honored and shamed her, she now began to command him so impatiently that her dissatisfaction with his obedience was already visible from the outset. Even though Mendel was not hard of hearing, Mrs. Skovronnek raised her voice to speak with him, as if she feared being misunderstood and as if she wanted to show through her shouting that Mendel often carried out her orders incorrectly because she had spoken to him in her usual register. Her shouting was a precautionary measure; the only thing that affronted Mendel. For he, who was so humiliated by heaven, made little of people's good-natured and careless mockery, and only when someone doubted his ability to understand was he offended. "Mendel, hurry up," thus began every order from Mrs. Skovronnek. He made her impatient, he seemed to her too slow. "Don't shout so," Mendel replied occasionally,

"I hear you." "But you're not hurrying, you're taking your time!" "I have less time than you, Mrs. Skovronnek, for I'm older than you!" Mrs. Skovronnek, who did not immediately comprehend the answer's connotation and the rebuke and only believed herself to have been mocked, turned immediately to the nearest person in the shop: "Well, what do you say to that? He's getting old! Our Mendel is getting old!" She would have gladly maligned him for entirely other qualities, but she settled for the mention of his age, which she regarded as a vice. When Skovronnek heard that sort of talk, he said to his wife: "We're all getting old! I am just as old as Mendel – and you're not getting any younger either!" "You can go ahead and marry a young woman," said Mrs. Skovronnek. She was happy that she finally had a ready-made reason for a marital dispute. And Mendel, who knew the development of these quarrels and comprehended from the beginning that Mrs. Skovronnek's rage would ultimately be vented against her husband and his friend, trembled for his friendship.

Today Mrs. Skovronnek was hostile toward Mendel for a particular reason. "Imagine," she said to her husband, "a few days ago my chopping knife disappeared. I can swear that Mendel took it. But when I ask him, he knows nothing about it. He's getting older and older, he's like a child!" In fact Mendel Singer had taken Mrs. Skovronnek's chopping knife and hidden it. He had long been secretly preparing a great plan, the last of his life. One evening he believed that he could carry it out. He pretended to fall asleep on the sofa while the neighbors talked at Skovronnek's.

But in reality Mendel wasn't sleeping at all. He was lying in wait and listening with closed eyelids until the last of them had left. Then he pulled out the chopping knife from under the pillow of the sofa, stuck it under his caftan and slipped into the evening street. The streetlamps were not yet lit, from some windows yellow lamplight already shone. Opposite the house in which he had lived with Deborah, Mendel Singer stood and peered at the windows of his former apartment. The young married couple Frisch now lived there, downstairs they had opened a modern ice cream parlor. Now the young people emerged from the house. They closed the parlor. They were going to a concert. They were frugal, stingy, one might say, industrious, and they loved music. Young Frisch's father had conducted a wedding band in Kovno. Today a concert was being given by a philharmonic orchestra, just come from Europe. Frisch had already been speaking about it for days. Now they were going. They didn't see Mendel. He crept across the street, entered the house, felt his way up the old familiar banister and pulled all the keys out of his pocket. He got them from the neighbors, who entrusted him with watching their apartments when they went to the movies. Without difficulty he opened the door. He locked the bolt, lay down flat on the floor and began to knock on one floorboard after another. It took a long time. He grew tired, granted himself a short break and then went back to work. Finally there came a hollow sound, just at the place where Deborah's bed once had stood. Mendel removed the dirt from the gaps, loosened the board at all four edges with the chopping knife and pried it up. He hadn't been mistaken, he found what he was looking for. He grasped the tightly knotted handkerchief, hid it in his caftan, replaced the board and left soundlessly. No one was in the stairwell, no one had seen him. Earlier than usual he locked the shop, he rolled down the shutters. He lit the large hanging lamp, the round burner, and sat down in its beam of light. He unknotted the handkerchief and counted its contents. Sixty-seven dollars in coins and bills Deborah had saved. It was a lot, but it was not enough and disappointed Mendel. If he added his own savings, the alms and small payments for his work in the houses, then he had exactly ninety-six dollars. That was not enough. "A few more months then!" Mendel whispered. "I have time."

Yes, he had time, he must go on living for quite a long time! Before him lay the great ocean. Once again he had to cross it. The whole great sea waited for Mendel. All of Zuchnow and its environs wait for him: the barracks, the pine forest, the frogs in the swamps and the crickets in the fields. If Menuchim is dead, he is lying in the small cemetery and waiting. Mendel too will lie down. First he will enter Sameshkin's farm, he will no longer fear the dogs, give him a wolf from Zuchnow, and he is not afraid. Heedless of the bugs and the worms, the tree frogs and the grasshoppers, Mendel will be able to lie down on the naked earth. The church bells will sound and remind him of the listening light in Menuchim's foolish eyes. Mendel will answer: "I have come home, dear Sameshkin, let others wander through the world, my worlds have died, I have returned to fall asleep here forever!" The blue night is stretched over the land, the stars are shining, the frogs are croaking, the crickets are chirping, and over there, in the dark forest, someone is singing Menuchim's song.

Thus Mendel falls asleep, in his hand he holds the knotted handkerchief.

The next morning he went to Skovronnek's apartment, lay the chopping knife on the cold kitchen stove and said: "Here, Mrs. Skovronnek, the chopping knife has turned up!"

He wanted to leave again quickly, but Mrs. Skovronnek began: "It has turned up! That wasn't hard, you hid it after all! By the way, you were fast asleep yesterday. We were outside the shop again and knocked. Did you hear? Frisch from the ice cream parlor has something very important to tell you. You should go over to him immediately."

Mendel was frightened. So someone had seen him yesterday, perhaps someone else had plundered the apartment, and they suspected Mendel. Or perhaps those weren't Deborah's savings at all, but Mrs. Frisch's, and he had robbed her. His knees trembled. "Permit me to sit down," he said to Mrs. Skovronnek. "For two minutes you can sit," she said, "then I have to cook." "What sort of important matter is it?" he probed. But he already knew that the woman would reveal nothing to him. She reveled in his curiosity and was silent. Then she thought the time had come to send him away. "I don't get involved in other people's business! Just go to Frisch!" she said. And Mendel left and resolved not to set foot in Frisch's. It could only be something bad. It would come on its own soon enough. He waited. But in the afternoon Skovronnek's grandchildren came to visit. Mrs. Skovronnek sent him for three portions of strawberry ice cream. Timidly Mendel entered the shop. Luckily Mr. Frisch wasn't there. His wife said: "My husband has something very important to tell you, you must come in the afternoon!"

Mendel acted as if he hadn't heard. His heart raced wildly, it wanted to flee him, with both hands he held it back. Something bad definitely threatened him. He wanted to tell the truth, Frisch would believe him. If no one believed him, he'd go to jail. Well, there was no harm in that. In jail he will die. Not in Zuchnow.

He couldn't leave the vicinity of the ice cream parlor. He walked up and down in front of the shop. He saw young Frisch return home. He wanted to wait longer, but his feet hastened by themselves into the shop. He opened the door, which set off a shrill bell, and no longer found the strength to close the door, so that the alarm incessantly sounded, and Mendel, deafened, remained trapped in its violent noise, captive to the ringing and incapable of moving. Mr. Frisch himself closed the door. And in the silence that now ensued, Mendel heard Mr. Frisch say to his wife: "Quick, a raspberry soda for Mr. Singer!"

How long had it been since anyone had called Mendel "Mr. Singer"? Not until that moment did he feel that people had long been calling him only "Mendel" so as to insult him. It is a mean joke of Frisch's, he thought. The whole neighborhood knows that this young man is stingy, he himself knows that I will not pay for the raspberry soda. I won't drink it.

"Thanks, thanks," said Mendel, "I won't have anything to drink!"

"You won't turn us down," the woman said with a smile.

"You won't turn me down," said young Frisch.

He pulled Mendel to one of the small thin-legged cast-iron tables and pushed the old man into a broad wicker chair. He himself sat down on an ordinary wooden chair, moved close to Mendel and began:

"Yesterday, Mr. Singer, I was, as you know, at a concert." Mendel's heart skipped a beat. He leaned back and took a sip, so as to keep himself alive. "Well," Frisch went on, "I've heard a lot of music, but there's never been anything like this before! Thirty-two musicians, you understand, and almost all of them from our region. And they played Jewish melodies, you understand? It warms the heart, I wept, the whole audience wept. At the end they played 'Menuchim's Song,' Mr. Singer, you know it from the gramophone. A beautiful song, isn't it?"

What does he want? thought Mendel. "Yes, yes, a beautiful song."

"During the intermission I go to the musicians. It's crowded. Everyone's pushing to the musicians. This person and that finds a friend, and I do too, Mr. Singer, I do too."

Frisch paused. People entered the shop, the bell rang shrilly.

"I find," said Mr. Frisch, "but drink, Mr. Singer! I find my cousin by blood, Berkovich from Kovno. The son of my uncle. And we kiss. And we talk. And suddenly Berkovich says: Do you know here an old man named Mendel Singer?"

Frisch waited again. But Mendel Singer didn't move. He took note of the fact that a certain Berkovich had asked after an old Mendel Singer.

"Yes," said Frisch, "I answered him that I know a Mendel Singer from Zuchnow. That's the one, said Berkovich. Our conductor is a great composer, still young and a genius, he wrote most of the pieces we play. His name is Alexei Kossak, and he is also from Zuchnow."

"Kossak?" Mendel repeated. "My wife was born a Kossak. He is a relative!"

"Yes," said Frisch, "and it seems that Kossak is looking for you. He probably wants to tell you something. And I am supposed to ask you whether you want to hear it. Either you can go to his hotel or I will write Berkovich your address."

Mendel felt light and heavy at the same time. He drank the raspberry soda, leaned back and said: "I thank you, Mr. Frisch. But it is not so important. This Kossak will tell me all the sad things I already know. And besides – I want to tell you the truth: I've already been meaning to consult with you. Your brother has a ship ticket agency, right? I want to go home, to Zuchnow. It is no longer Russia, the world has changed. What does a ship ticket cost these days? And what sorts of papers do I need? Talk to your brother, but don't tell anyone else."

"I'll inquire," replied Frisch. "But you certainly don't have enough money. And at your age! Maybe this Kossak will tell you something! Maybe he'll take you with him! He's only staying for a short time in New York! Shall I give Berkovich your address? Because, if I know you, you won't go to the hotel!"

"No," said Mendel, "I won't go. Write to him if you wish."

He rose.

Frisch pushed him back into the chair. "One moment," he said, "Mr. Singer, I've brought along the program. Here is the picture of this Kossak." And he pulled from his breast pocket a large program, unfolded it and held it before Mendel's eyes.

"A good-looking young man," said Mendel. He gazed at the photograph. Even though the picture was worn, the paper dirty, and the portrait seemed to dissolve into a hundred thousand tiny molecules, it came alive from the program before Mendel's eyes. He wanted to give it back immediately, but he kept it and stared at it. Broad and white was the forehead under the black of the hair, like a smooth sunlit stone. The eyes were large and bright. They looked straight at Mendel Singer, he could no longer free himself from them. They made him joyful and light, Mendel believed. He saw their intelligence shining. They were at once old and young. They knew everything, the world was reflected in them. Mendel Singer felt as if he himself became younger at the sight of those eyes, he became a youth, he knew nothing at all. He had to learn everything from those eyes. He has already seen them, dreamed them, as a small boy. Years ago, when he began to study the Bible, they were the eyes of the prophets. Men to whom God himself has spoken have those eyes. They know everything, they reveal nothing, the light is in them.

For a long time Mendel looked at the picture. Then he said: "I will take it home with me, if you permit, Mr. Frisch." And he folded up the paper and left. He went around the corner, unfolded the program, looked at it and pocketed it again. A long time seemed to have passed since the hour he entered the ice cream parlor. The few thousand years that shone in Kossak's eyes lay between, and the years since Mendel had still been so young that he had been able to imagine the faces of prophets. He wanted to turn around, ask about the concert hall where the orchestra played and go there. But he felt ashamed. He entered the Skovronneks' shop and told them that a relative of his wife's was looking for him in America. He had given Frisch permission to pass on his address.

"Tomorrow evening you will eat with us, as you do every year," said Skovronnek. It was the first Easter evening. Mendel nodded. He would rather stay in his back room, he knew the sidelong glances of Mrs. Skovronnek and the calculating hands with which she portioned out to Mendel the soup and fish. "It is the last time," he thought. "A year from now I will be in Zuchnow, alive or dead, preferably dead."

He was the first guest to arrive the next evening, but the last to sit down at the table. He came early to avoid offending Mrs. Skovronnek, he took his seat late to show that he regarded himself as the lowliest among those present. They already sat around the table: the housewife, both of Skovronnek's daughters with their husbands and children, a strange traveling music supplies salesman and Mendel. He sat at the end of the table, on which a planed board had been laid to extend it. Mendel was worried not only about the preservation of peace but also about the balance between the tabletop and its artificial extension. Mendel held the end of the board with one hand when someone had to put a plate or a tureen on it. Six thick snow-white candles burned in six silver candlesticks on the snow-white tablecloth, the starched glow of which reflected back the six flames. Like white and silver guards of equal height the candles stood before Skovronnek, the man of the house, who sat in a white robe on a white pillow, leaning on another pillow, a sinless king on a sinless throne. How long ago had it been when Mendel had reigned over the table and the feast in the same costume, in the same fashion? Today he sat bowed and beaten, in his green shimmering coat at the farthest end, the lowliest among the guests, anxious about his own humility and a pitiful support for the celebration. The Easter bread lay covered under a white napkin, a snowy hill next to the lush green of the herbs, the dark red of the beets and the bitter yellow of the horseradish root. The books with the accounts of the exodus of the Jews from Egypt lay open before each guest. Skovronnek began to sing the legend, and everyone repeated his words, caught up with him and sang harmoniously in chorus that cozy, smiling melody, an enumeration in song of the individual miracles that were tallied again and again and yielded again and again the same qualities of God: the greatness, the goodness, the mercifulness, the grace for Israel and the wrath against Pharaoh. Even the music supplies salesman, who could not read the scripture and did not understand the customs, could not escape the melody, which with each new verse wooed, ensnared and caressed him, so that he began to hum along without knowing it. And even Mendel it made mild toward heaven, which four thousand years ago had generously bestowed joyful miracles, and it was as if, through God's love for the whole people, Mendel was almost reconciled with his own small fate. Still he didn't sing along, Mendel Singer, but his upper body swung forward and back, rocked by the singing of the others. He heard Skovronnek's grandchildren singing with high voices and remembered the voices of his own children. He still saw the helpless Menuchim on the unfamiliar raised chair at the ceremonial table. Only the father, from time to time during the singing, had cast a quick glance at his youngest and poorest son, seen the listening light in his foolish eyes and felt how the little one strove in vain to convey what sounded in him and to sing what he heard. It was the only evening in the year when Menuchim wore a new coat, like his brothers, and the white collar of the shirt with the brick red pattern as a festive border around his flabby double chin. When Mendel held out the wine to him, he drank half the cup with a greedy gulp, gasped and snorted and contorted his face in a failed attempt to laugh or to cry: who could know.

Mendel thought of that as he rocked to the singing of the others. He saw that they were already far ahead, turned a few pages and prepared to stand up, to disburden the corner of the plates so that no accident would occur when he let go. For the moment was approaching when the red goblet would be filled with wine and the door opened to let in the prophet Eliyahu. The dark red glass was already waiting, the six lights were reflected in its curve. Mrs. Skovronnek lifted her head and looked at Mendel. He stood up, shuffled to the door and opened it. Skovronnek now sang the invitation to the prophet. Mendel waited until it was over. For he didn't want to make the trip twice. Then he closed the door, sat back down, braced the supporting fist under the table board, and the singing went on.

Scarcely a minute after Mendel had sat down, there was a knock. Everyone heard the knock, but everyone thought it was an illusion. On that evening all their friends were sitting at home, the streets of the neighborhood were empty. At that hour no visit was possible. It was surely the wind knocking. "Mendel," said Mrs. Skovronnek, "you didn't close the door correctly." Then there was another knock, distinct and longer. Everyone paused. The smell of the candles, the pleasure of the wine, the yellow unfamiliar light and the old melody had brought the adults and the children so close to the anticipation of a miracle that they stopped breathing for a moment and looked at one another, helpless and pale, as if they wanted to ask whether the prophet wasn't really demanding admittance. Thus it remained silent, and no one dared move. Finally Mendel stirred. Again he pushed the plates into the middle. Again he shuffled to the door and opened it. There stood a tall stranger in the half-dark hallway, wished him a good evening and asked whether he might enter. Skovronnek rose with some difficulty from his pillows. He went to the door, observed the stranger and said: "Please!" – as he had learned to do in America. The stranger entered. He wore a dark coat, his collar was turned up, he kept his hat on his head, apparently out of reverence for the ceremony he had come upon, and because all the men there sat with covered heads.

He is a fine man, thought Skovronnek. And he unbuttoned, without saying a word, the stranger's coat. The man bowed and said: "My name is Alexei Kossak. I beg your pardon. I sincerely beg your pardon. I was told that a certain Mendel Singer from Zuchnow is staying with you. I would like to speak to him."

"That is I," said Mendel, approached the guest and lifted his head. His forehead reached to the stranger's shoulder. "Mr. Kossak," Mendel went on, "I've heard about you. You are a relative."

"Take off your coat and sit down with us at the table," said Skovronnek.

Mrs. Skovronnek rose. Everyone pushed together. They made space for the stranger. Skovronnek's son-in-law brought another chair to the table. The stranger hung his coat on a nail and sat down opposite Mendel. A cup of wine was set before the guest. "Don't let me hold you up," implored Kossak, "go on praying."

They continued. Quiet and slender the guest sat in his place. Mendel gazed at him incessantly. Tirelessly Alexei Kossak looked at Mendel Singer. Thus they sat opposite each other, enveloped by the singing of the others but separated from them.

They both found it pleasant that, because of the others, they could not yet speak to each other. Mendel sought the eyes of the stranger. If Kossak lowered them, the old man felt as if he had to implore the guest to keep them open. In that face everything was strange to Mendel Singer, only the eyes behind the rimless glasses were close to him. To them his gaze strayed again and again, as if in a homecoming to familiar lights hidden behind windows, from the foreign landscape of the thin, pale and youthful face. Thin, closed and smooth were the lips. If I were his father, thought Mendel, I would tell him: "Smile, Alexei." Softly he pulled out of his pocket the poster, unfolded it under the table to avoid disturbing the others, and handed it to the stranger. He took it and smiled, thinly, delicately and for only a second.

The singing stopped, the feast began, Mrs. Skovronnek pushed a bowl of hot soup before the guest, and Mr. Skovronnek invited him to eat with them. The music supplies salesman began a conversation in English with Kossak, of which Mendel understood nothing at all. Then the salesman declared to everyone that Kossak was a young genius, was staying only another week in New York and would take the liberty of sending everyone here free tickets to the concert of his orchestra. Other conversations could not start. They ate in barely festive haste to the end of the celebration, and every other bite was accompanied by a polite word from the stranger or his hosts. Mendel didn't speak. To please Mrs. Skovronnek he ate still faster than the others, so as not to cause any delays. And everyone welcomed the end of the meal and eagerly continued the singing of the miracles. Skovronnek struck an ever-faster rhythm, the women couldn't follow him. But when he came to the psalms, he changed his voice, the tempo and the melody, and so beguiling sounded the words he now sang that even Mendel, at the end of each verse, repeated "Hallelujah, hallelujah!" He shook his head so that his long beard swept over the open pages of the book and a soft rustle was audible, as if Mendel's beard wanted to participate in the prayer, because Mendel's mouth celebrated so sparingly.

Now they were almost finished. The candles had burned down halfway, the table was no longer smooth and ceremonial, there were stains and food scraps on the white tablecloth, and Skovronnek's grandchildren were already yawning. They stopped at the end of the book. Skovronnek said with a raised voice the traditional wish: "Next year in Jerusalem!" Everyone repeated it, closed the books and turned to the guest. It was now Mendel's turn to question the visitor. The old man cleared his throat, smiled and said: "Well, Mr. Alexei, what do you want to tell me?"

In a low voice the stranger began: "You would have heard from me long ago, Mr. Mendel Singer, if I had known your address. But after the war no one knew it any longer. Billes's son-in-law, the musician, died of typhus, your house in Zuchnow stood empty, because Billes's daughter had fled to her parents, who were then living in Dubno already, and in Zuchnow, in your house, were Austrian soldiers. Now, after the war I wrote to my manager here, but the man was not skilled enough, he wrote to me that you could not be found."

"A shame about Billes's son-in-law!" said Mendel, and he thought of Menuchim.

"And now," Kossak went on, "I have pleasant news." Mendel lifted his head. "I've bought your house, from old Billes, before witnesses and on the basis of an official appraisal. And I want to pay you the money."

"How much is it?" asked Mendel.

"Three hundred dollars!" said Kossak.

Mendel grasped his beard and combed it with spread trembling fingers. "I thank you!" he said. "And as for your son Jonas," Kossak went on, "he has been missing since 1915. No one could say anything about him. Neither in Petersburg nor in Berlin, nor in Vienna, nor at the Swiss Red Cross. I have inquired and had inquiries made everywhere. But two months ago I met a young man from Moscow. He had just come as a refugee across the Polish border, for as you know, Zuchnow now belongs to Poland. And this young man had been Jonas's comrade in the regiment. He told me that he once heard by chance that Jonas is alive and is fighting in the White Army. Now it has certainly become very hard to learn anything about him. But you must not give up hope yet."

Mendel was about to open his mouth to ask about Menuchim. But his friend Skovronnek, who anticipated Mendel's question, regarded a sad answer as certain and was anxious to avoid gloomy conversations that evening or at least to postpone them as long as possible, preempted the old man and said: "Now, Mr. Kossak, since we have the pleasure of having such a great man as yourself with us, perhaps you will also give us the joy of hearing something about your life. How has it come about that you have survived the war, the revolution and all the dangers?"

The stranger had apparently not been expecting that question, for he did not answer immediately. He lowered his eyes, like someone who feels ashamed or has to think, and only answered after a long while: "I haven't experienced anything special. As a child I was sick for a long time, my father was a poor teacher, like Mr. Mendel Singer, to whose wife I am related. (Now is not the time to explain the relation in more detail.) In short, due to my illness, and because we were poor, I ended up in a big city, in a public medical institute. They treated me well, a doctor was particularly fond of me, I recovered, and the doctor kept me in his house. There," here Kossak lowered his voice and his head, and it was as if he were speaking to the table, so that all held their breath so as to hear him clearly, "there I sat down one day at the piano and played from my head my own songs. And the doctor's wife wrote the notes to my songs. The war was my good fortune. For I came to military music and became the conductor of a band, stayed the whole time in Petersburg and played a few times for the Tsar. After the revolution my band went abroad with me. A few left, a few new ones joined, in London we signed a contract with a concert agency, and thus my orchestra came to be."

Everyone was still listening, even though the guest had long since finished his story. But his words still hovered in the room, and the listeners were only now struck by them. Kossak spoke the jargon of the Jews poorly, he mixed half Russian sentences in his story, and the Skovronneks and Mendel did not comprehend them individually, but only in the whole context. Skovronnek's sons-in-law, who had come to America as small children, only understood half of it and had their wives translate the stranger's story into English for them. The music supplies salesman then repeated Kossak's biography so as to memorize it. The candles were still burning only as short stumps in the candlesticks, it grew dark in the room, the grandchildren were sleeping with inclined heads in their chairs, but no one made a move to go, indeed Mrs. Skovronnek even fetched two new candles, stuck them on the old stumps and thus reopened the evening. Her old respect for Mendel Singer awakened. This guest, who was a great man, had played for the Tsar, wore a remarkable ring on his little finger and a pearl in his tie, was dressed in a suit of good European fabric – she knew about that because her father had been a clothier – this guest could not go with Mendel into the back room of the shop. Indeed she said to her husband's surprise:

"Mr. Singer! It is good that you have come to us this evening. Usually," and she turned to Kossak, "he is so humble and tactful that he declines all my invitations. Nonetheless, he is like the oldest child in our house." Skovronnek interrupted her: "Make us some more tea!" And as she stood up, he said to Kossak: "We've all known your songs for a long time. 'Menuchim's Song' is by you, isn't it?" "Yes," said Kossak. "It is by me." It seemed that this question displeased him. He quickly looked at Mendel Singer and asked: "Your wife is dead?" Mendel nodded. "And as far as I know, you have a daughter, don't you?" Instead of Mendel Skovronnek now answered: "Unfortunately the deaths of her mother and her brother Sam drove her mad, and she is in the asylum." The stranger lowered his head again. Mendel rose.

He wanted to ask about Menuchim, but he did not have the courage. He knew the answer already. He put himself in the guest's place and answered himself: Menuchim is long dead. He died miserably. He impressed this sentence on himself, tasted in advance its whole bitterness, so that, when the sentence should actually sound, he could remain calm. And because he still felt a shy hope stirring deep in his heart, he sought to kill it. If Menuchim were alive, he said to himself, the stranger would have told me right at the outset. No! Menuchim is long dead. Now I will ask him, so that this stupid hope will come to an end! But he still didn't ask. He took a pause, and the noisy activity of Mrs. Skovronnek, who was busy with the tea maker in the kitchen, prompted him to leave the room, so as to help the housewife, as he was accustomed.

But today she sent him back into the room. He had three hundred dollars and a noble relative. "It isn't proper for you, Mr. Mendel," she said. "Don't leave your guest alone!" She was already finished anyhow. With the full tea glasses on the broad tray she entered the room, followed by Mendel. The tea steamed. Mendel was finally determined to ask about Menuchim. Skovronnek too felt that the question could no longer be postponed. He preferred to ask it himself, Mendel, his friend, should not, on top of the pain the answer would cause him, have to take on himself the torment of asking.

"My friend Mendel had another poor sick son named Menuchim. What has happened to him?"

Again the stranger didn't answer. He poked around with the spoon on the bottom of his glass, ground the sugar, and as if he wanted to read the answer in the tea, he looked at the light brown glass and, the spoon still between his thumb and forefinger, his slender brown hand gently moving, he finally said, unexpectedly loudly, as if with a sudden resolution:

"Menuchim is alive!"

It doesn't sound like an answer, it sounds like a cry. Immediately a laugh bursts from Mendel Singer's breast. Everyone is startled and stares at the old man. Mendel is sitting in the chair, leaning back, shaking and laughing. His back is so bowed that it cannot entirely touch the backrest. Between the backrest and the nape of Mendel's old neck (little white hairs curl over the shabby collar of his coat) is a wide gap. Mendel's long beard moves violently, almost flutters like a white flag and seems itself to be laughing. From Mendel's breast roars and giggles come alternately. Everyone is startled, Skovronnek rises somewhat laboriously from the swelling pillows, hampered by the long white robe, and walks around the whole table, approaches Mendel, bends down to him and takes Mendel's two hands in his. Then Mendel's laughter turns into weeping, he sobs, and the tears flow from the old half-veiled eyes into the rampant beard, lose themselves in the wild underbrush, others get caught for a long time, round and full like glass drops, in the hair.

Finally Mendel is calm. He looks straight at Kossak and repeats: "Menuchim is alive?"

The stranger looks at Mendel calmly and says: "Menuchim is alive, he is healthy, and he is even doing well!"

Mendel folds his hands, he lifts them as high as he can toward the ceiling. He would like to stand up. He has the feeling that he should now stand up, straighten up, grow, become taller and taller, rise above the house and touch the sky with his hands. He can no longer unclasp his folded hands. He looks at Skovronnek, and his old friend knows what he now has to ask in Mendel's stead.

"Where is Menuchim now?" asks Skovronnek.

And slowly Alexei Kossak replies:

"I myself am Menuchim."

All rise suddenly from their seats, the children, who were already asleep, awake and burst into tears. Mendel himself stands up so violently that behind him the chair falls down with a loud crash. He walks, he runs, he hastens, he skips to Kossak, the only one who has remained sitting. There is a great uproar in the room. The candles begin to flicker as if they were suddenly stirred by a wind. On the walls flutter the shadows of standing people. Mendel sinks down before the sitting Menuchim, he seeks with anxious mouth and waving beard the hands of his son, his lips kiss whatever they meet, the knees, the thighs, the vest of Menuchim. Mendel stands up again, lifts his hands and begins, as if he had suddenly gone blind, with eager fingers to touch his son's face. The blunt old fingers glide over Menuchim's hair, his smooth broad forehead, the cold lenses of his glasses, the thin closed lips. Menuchim sits calmly and doesn't move. All the guests surround Menuchim and Mendel, the children weep, the candles flicker, the shadows on the wall amass into heavy clouds. No one speaks.

Finally Menuchim's voice sounds. "Stand up, Father!" he says, and grasps Mendel under his arms, lifts him up and sits him on his lap, as if he were a child. The others withdraw again. Now Mendel sits on his son's lap, smiles all around, in everyone's face. He whispers: "Pain will make him wise, ugliness kind, bitterness gentle, and illness strong." Deborah said that. He still hears her voice. Skovronnek leaves the table, takes off his robe, puts on his coat and says: "I'll be right back!" Where is Skovronnek going? It is not yet late, not even eleven o'clock, their friends are still sitting at their tables. He goes from house to house, to Groschel, Menkes and Rottenberg. They can all still be found at their tables. "A miracle has happened! Come with me and see it!" He leads all three to Mendel. On the way they meet Lemmel's daughter, who was accompanying her guests. They tell her about Mendel and Menuchim. Young Frisch, who is going for a little walk with his wife, also hears the news. Thus a few people learn what has occurred. Down below outside Skovronnek's house stands, as proof, the automobile in which Menuchim has come. A few people open their windows and see it. Menkes, Groschel, Skovrennek and Rottenberg enter the house. Mendel comes to meet them and silently squeezes their hands.

Menkes, the most thoughtful of them all, spoke. "Mendel," he said, "we have come to see you in your good luck as we have seen you in misfortune. Do you remember how you were beaten? We consoled you, but we knew it was in vain. Now you are experiencing a miracle in the living flesh. As we were sad with you then, today we are joyful with you. Great are the miracles that the Eternal One performs, still today, as several thousand years ago. Praised be His name!" All stood. Skovronnek's daughters, the children, the sons-in-law and the music supplies salesman were already in their coats and said goodbye. Mendel's friends didn't sit down, because they had come only to offer their brief congratulations. Smaller than all of them, with a hunched back, in a green shimmering coat, Mendel stood in their midst like an inconspicuously disguised king. He had to stretch to look into their faces. "I thank you," he said. "Without your help I would not have lived to see this hour. Look at my son!" He pointed to him with his hand, as if one of his friends might not observe Menuchim thoroughly enough. Their eyes felt the fabric of the suit, the silk tie, the pearl, the slender hands and the ring. Then they said: "A noble young man! One sees that he is special!"

"I have no house," Mendel said to his son. "You come to your father, and I don't know where to offer you a bed."

"I would like to take you with me, Father," the son replied. "I don't know whether you are allowed to drive, because it is a holiday."

"He's allowed to drive," said everyone, as if with one mouth.

"I believe that I am allowed to drive with you," declared Mendel. "I have committed grave sins, the Lord has closed his eyes. I have called him an *ispravnik*. He has covered his ears. He is so great that our badness becomes very small. I am allowed to drive with you."

All accompanied Mendel to the car. At this window and that neighbors stood and looked down. Mendel fetched his keys, unlocked the shop again, went into the back room and took the little red velvet sack from the nail. He blew on it to free it from the dust, rolled down the shutters, locked up and gave Skovronnek the keys. Holding the sack, he climbed into the car. The engine rattled. The headlights shone. From this window and that voices called: "Goodbye, Mendel." Mendel Singer grasped Menkes by the sleeve and said: "Tomorrow, at the prayer, you will announce that I am donating three hundred dollars to the poor. Farewell!"

And he drove at his son's side to Forty-fourth and Broadway, the Astor Hotel.

XVI

Pitiful and stooped, in a green shimmering coat, holding the little red velvet sack, Mendel Singer entered the lobby, observed the electric light, the blond porter, the white bust of an unknown god at the foot of the stairs and the black Negro who tried to take the sack from him. He stepped into the elevator and saw himself in the mirror next to his son, he closed his eyes, for he felt dizzy. He had already died, he was floating in heaven, it would never end. His son grasped him by the hand, the elevator stopped, Mendel walked on a soundless carpet through a long corridor. He didn't open his eyes until he stood in the room. As was his wont, he went immediately to the window. There he saw for the first time the American night from up close, the reddened sky, the flaming, sparkling, dripping, glowing, red, blue, green, silver, golden letters, pictures and signs. He heard the noisy song of America, the honking, the tooting, the roaring, the ringing, the screeching, the creaking, the whistling and the howling. Opposite the window on which Mendel was leaning appeared every five seconds the broad laughing face of a girl, composed entirely of sprayed sparks and points, the blinding teeth in the open mouth made of a piece of melted silver. A ruby red, foaming goblet floated toward this face, tipped of its own accord, poured its contents into the open mouth and withdrew, to reappear newly filled, ruby red and foaming over with white froth. It was an advertisement for a new soda. Mendel admired it as the most perfect representation of the night's happiness and of golden health. He smiled, watched the picture come and disappear a few times and turned back to the room. There stood his white bed with the covers turned back. Menuchim was rocking in a rocking chair. "I won't sleep tonight," said Mendel. "You lie down to sleep, I'll sit beside you. You slept in the corner, in Zuchnow, next to the stove." "I remember clearly one day," began Menuchim, taking off his glasses, and Mendel saw the naked eyes of his son, they seemed to him sad and weary, "I remember a morning, the sun is very bright, the room empty. Then you come, lift me up, I sit on a table, and you ring a glass with a spoon. It was a wonderful ring, I wish I could compose and play it today. Then you sing. Then the clocks begin to toll, very old ones, like great heavy spoons they strike gigantic glasses." "Go on, go on," said Mendel. He too remembered clearly that day, on which Deborah left the house to prepare for the journey to Kapturak. "That's the only thing from the early days!" said his son. "Then comes the time when Billes's son-in-law, the violinist, plays. Every day, I believe, he plays. He stops playing, but I always hear him, all day long, all night long." "Go on, go on!" urged Mendel, in the tone in which he always encouraged his pupils to study.

"Then there's nothing for a long time! Then one day I see a great red and blue fire. I lie down on the floor. I crawl to the door. Suddenly someone pulls me up and pushes me, I run. I'm outside, people are standing on the other side of the street. Fire! The cry bursts from me!" "Go on, go on!" urged Mendel. "I remember nothing else. They told me later that I was sick and unconscious for a long time. I remember only the times in Petersburg, a white hall, white beds, many children in the beds, a harmonium or an organ is playing, and I sing along with a loud voice. Then the doctor takes me home in a car. A tall blond woman in a pale blue dress is playing piano. She stands up. I go to the keys, there's a sound when I touch them. Suddenly I play the songs of the organ and everything I can sing." "Go on, go on!" urged Mendel. "I can think of nothing else that would matter more to me than those few days. I remember my mother. It was warm and soft with her, I believe she had a very deep voice, and her face was very big and round, like a whole world." "Go on, go on!" said Mendel. "Miriam, Jonas, Shemariah I don't remember. I heard about them only much later, from Billes's daughter."

Mendel sighed. "Miriam," he repeated. She stood before him, in her golden-yellow shawl, with her blue-black hair, nimble and light-footed, a young gazelle. She had his eyes. "I was a bad father," said Mendel. "I treated you badly, and her too. Now she is lost, no medicine can help her." "We will go to her," said Menuchim. "I myself, Father, have I not been healed?"

Yes, Menuchim was right. Man is unsatisfied, Mendel said to himself. He has just experienced a miracle, already he wants to see the next. Wait, wait, Mendel Singer! Just look what has become of Menuchim, the cripple. Slender are his hands, wise are his eyes, soft are his cheeks.

"Go to sleep, Father!" said his son. He sat down on the floor and pulled off Mendel Singer's old boots. He gazed at the soles, which were torn, had jagged edges, the yellow patched uppers, the roughened shafts, the hole-riddled socks, the frayed pants. He undressed the old man and laid him in bed. Then he left the room, took a book from his suitcase, returned to his father, sat down in the rocking chair next to the bed, lit the small green lamp and began to read. Mendel pretended to sleep. He squinted through a narrow crack between his eyelids. His son laid the book aside and said: "You are thinking of Miriam, Father! We will visit her. I will call doctors. They will cure her. She is still young! Go to sleep!" Mendel closed his eyes, but he didn't fall asleep. He thought of Miriam, heard the unfamiliar noises of the world, felt through his closed eyelids the nocturnal flames of the bright sky. He didn't sleep, but he felt at ease, he rested. With his wakeful head he lay bedded in sleep and waited for the morning.

His son prepared him a bath, dressed him, sat him in the car. They drove for a long time through noisy streets, they left the city, they came to a long and wide road, on the sides of which stood budding trees. The engine emitted a high-pitched hum, in the wind Mendel's beard waved. He was silent. "Do you want to know where we're going, Father?" asked his son. "No!" answered Mendel. "I don't want to know anything! Wherever you go is good."

And they reached a world where the soft sand was yellow, the wide sea blue and all the houses white. On the terrace in front of one of those houses, at a small white table, sat Mendel Singer. He slurped a golden-brown tea. On his stooped back shone the first warm sun of the year. The blackbirds hopped up close to him. Their sisters were fluting in front of the terrace. The waves of the sea lapped the shore with a gentle regular beat. In the pale blue sky were a few little white clouds. Under that sky Mendel was willing to believe that Jonas would one day turn up again and Miriam come home, "in all the land were no women found so fair," he quoted inwardly. He himself, Mendel Singer, will, after late years, have a good death, surrounded by many grandchildren and "old and full of days," as it was written in "Job." He felt a strange and also forbidden longing to take off the cap of old silk rep and let the sun shine on his old pate. And for the first time in his life Mendel Singer voluntarily uncovered his head, as he had done only in an office or in the bath. The sparse, curly little hairs on his bald head were moved by a spring wind, as if they were strange delicate plants.

Thus Mendel Singer greeted the world.

And a gull flew, like a silver bullet of the sky, under the canopy of the terrace. Mendel watched its precipitous flight and the shadowy white trail that it left behind in the blue air.

Then the son said:

"Next week I'm going to San Francisco. On the way back we're playing ten days in Chicago. I think, Father, that we can go to Europe in four weeks!"

"Miriam?"

"Today I will see her, talk to doctors. Everything will be fine,

Father. Maybe we will take her with us. Maybe she will recover in Europe!"

They returned to the hotel. Mendel went into his son's room. He was tired. "Lie down on the sofa, sleep a little," said his son. "In two hours I'll be back!"

Mendel lay down obediently. He knew where his son was going. He was going to his sister. He was a wonderful man, the blessing rested on him, he would make Miriam healthy.

Mendel glimpsed a large photograph in a reddish-brown frame on the small dressing table. "Give me the picture!" he implored.

He gazed at it for a long time. He saw the young blond woman in a bright dress, bright as the day, she sat in a garden, through which the wind meandered and moved the bushes at the edges of the flowerbeds. Two children, a girl and a boy, stood next to a small wagon with a donkey harnessed to it, as are used in some gardens as a vehicle for play.

"God bless them!" said Mendel.

The son left. The father remained on the sofa, he laid the photograph gently beside him. His weary eyes wandered through the room to the window. From his deep sofa he could see a jagged cloudless piece of sky. He picked up the picture again. There was his daughter-in-law, Menuchim's wife, there were his grandchildren, Menuchim's children. When he looked at the girl more closely, he thought he saw a childhood picture of Deborah. Dead was Deborah, with strange, otherworldly eyes she perhaps witnessed the miracle. Gratefully Mendel remembered her young warmth, which he had once tasted, her red cheeks, her half-open eyes, which had shone in the dark nights of love, narrow enticing lights. Dead Deborah!

He stood up, pushed a chair to the sofa, placed the picture on the chair and lay down again. As they slowly closed, his eyes took the whole blue brightness of the sky into sleep and the faces of the new children. Beside them emerged from the portrait's brown background Jonas and Miriam. Mendel fell asleep. And he rested from the weight of happiness and the greatness of miracles.

Translator's Afterword

"I've seen a few worlds perish," laments Mendel Singer, the protagonist of Joseph Roth's 1930 novel *Job: The Story of a Simple Man*, in the course of a life afflicted by one misfortune after another. So too had his creator. Born in 1894 in Brody, a small, mostly Jewish town in Galicia – a province at the easternmost edge of the Austro-Hungarian Empire, six miles from the Russian border – Roth witnessed the disappearance of his homeland from the map with the dissolution of the Habsburg monarchy in 1918. This experience of irretrievable loss through historic upheaval profoundly shaped his fiction, essays and journalism. Above all, his twin masterpieces – *Job*, the tale of an uprooted Russian Jew, and *The Radetzky March* (1932), a generational novel that traces Austria-Hungary's demise – convey the fundamental homesickness at the heart of the author's life and work.

When Roth first left home in 1913 for the University of Lemberg, from which he transferred the following year to the University of Vienna, he was not eager to identify with his origins. Indeed, as a student in the Austrian capital – where there was widespread contempt for *Ostjuden*, as Eastern European Jews were disparagingly called, and Galicia was considered a particularly backward region – he sought to disguise his background through false biographical claims and affectations. He named Schwaben-dorf, a predominantly German town, as his birthplace, and variously described his father – who in reality had been placed in care for madness before Joseph was born – as a Viennese factory owner, an army officer, a Polish aristocrat, and other imaginary figures. In 1916 Roth abandoned his German literature studies to volunteer for military service in the First World War. Upon entering the anti-Semitic atmosphere of the Austrian Army, he shed his former first name, Moses (Joseph had been his middle name).

The fall of the empire at the end of the war became the pivotal event of Roth's life. His novels of the early 1920s are *Heimkehrerromane*, stories about returning soldiers. They testify to the shock of his own unattainable homecoming. Like the writer himself, Roth's soldiers invariably discover that, in the radically transformed postwar landscape, they no longer have homes to come back to. Though he moved to Berlin in 1923 with his new wife – Friederike Reichler, the daughter of Galician-Jewish parents – Roth went on to lead a restless, itinerant existence as a journalist for Austrian and German newspapers, usually of a liberal or leftist bent. As a foreign correspondent, he reported from a variety of places, including Russia, Poland, Albania, Italy and France. His was the life of a stateless nomad, shuttling among the hotels, cafés and taverns of Europe's cities and provinces. Fittingly for a man of the press, his debut as a novelist in 1923, *The Spider's Web* – which presciently diagnosed the threat of the fascist right – was published as a newspaper serial.

In keeping with Roth's journalistic activity, his early novels – such as *Hotel Savoy* (1924), *Rebellion* (1924), *Zipper and His Father* (1928), and *Right and Left* (1929) – are observational accounts of such subjects as the return from war, political unrest, and the failed search for personal fulfillment amid the harsh realities of postwar Europe. They largely exemplify the principles of the *Neue Sachlichkeit* (New Objectivity), an aesthetic and literary movement of 1920s Germany that emerged in opposition to the emotiveness of Expressionism and championed documentary-style portrayals of social conditions, often with a political edge. Notable among the representative works of the movement are the art of George Grosz, the photography of August Sander, and the writing of Alfred Döblin, which share a commitment to raw depictions of contemporary life. Roth articulates a similar approach in his preface to his 1927 novel *Flight Without End*: "I have invented nothing, composed nothing. It is no longer a matter of 'poetic creation.' What is most important is what is observed."

Job marks a turning point in Roth's career. In it, he ventures into the depths of inner subjectivity so as to convey the vicissitudes of an individual fate. As the title suggests, the tale of Mendel Singer, a pious, destitute and "entirely everyday" children's Torah teacher whose faith is tested at every turn, is a modern fable based on the Biblical story of Job. Singer witnesses the collapse of his world: his youngest son is born with what seem to be incurable disabilities, one of his older sons joins the Russian Army, the other deserts to America, and his daughter is running around with a Cossack. When he flees to America with his wife and daughter, further blows await him. Ultimately, in the face of unbearable suffering and loss, Singer gives up hope and curses God, only to be saved by a miraculous reversal of fortune. A stirring exploration of the human heart in its most profound sorrows and joys, *Job* achieves a new artistic height in Roth's oeuvre, displaying the poetic potency and sensitivity that would henceforth characterize his writing.

But the novelist, in entering this later phase, did not abandon his extraordinary powers of realism. In his description of the shtetl where the story begins, for example, Roth renders in luminous detail the milieu with which he was familiar from his Galician childhood and which he documented in 1927 in a collection of journalistic essays on Eastern European Jewry titled *The Wandering Jews*. Roth's interest in those who had been displaced by the redrawing of national boundaries – in the wake of the war, the Russian Revolution and the Treaty of Versailles – extended beyond Jewish refugees. He wrote dispatches from encampments and ghettos in which unwelcome, maltreated people of all sorts dwelled. Nonetheless, it is no wonder that the centuries-old figure of the migrant Jew who is nowhere at home would strike the writer as an embodiment of the peripatetic nature of postwar modern life, ultimately prompting him to evoke the trope of Jewish exile in *Job*. Roth's firsthand encounters did not merely provide *Job* with realistic detail, but also enhanced his intimacy with a deeper current of Jewish experience. As a stranger everywhere himself, he must have felt all the more attuned to the Jewish condition of rootlessness, encapsulated by the Russian peasant Sameshkin in *Job* with little sympathy: "Why do you people always roam around so much in the world! The devil sends you from one place to another."

In its combination of Roth's well-honed reportorial exactitude with a newfound melancholy lyricism, *Job* anticipates *The Radetzky March*, the author's elegy for the Austro-Hungarian Empire. There is also a connection between the subjects of the two works: Roth's increasing nostalgia for the monarchy was intimately related to his consciousness of Jewish homelessness. Roth was one of many Austro-Hungarian Jews who had embraced the imperial ideal of a supranational, multiethnic state. However imperfect its realization, this ideal offered the monarchy's Jewish subjects, who could not claim a territory of their own, a promise of belonging. The breakup of the Empire – precipitated by the national independence movements of Czechs, Slovaks, Poles, Ukrainians, Serbs, Croats and Slovenes – shattered this hope and gave rise to nation-states based on ethnicity in which Jews were imperiled by greater marginalization and persecution.

Roth's mourning for the bygone era of his early years forms the thematic core of his work. Certain motifs drawn from his Galician memories turn up again and again in passages tinged with sorrow. One such moment occurs in *Job*, when a few scarcely discernible stars over Manhattan remind Singer of "the bright starry nights at home, the deep blue of the widely spanning sky, the gently curved sickle of the moon, the dark rustle of the pines in the forest, the voices of the crickets and frogs." These are the sights and sounds of Roth's childhood surroundings. Similarly recurrent is a cast of characters: smugglers and deserters, Hassidic "wonder rabbis" and fleeing Jews, tavern keepers and middlemen, Cossacks and Ruthenian peasants, Polish nobles and Austrian officers – all the mysterious borderland figures that fascinated the young Roth in Brody. They populate his stories and play important roles in *Job* and *The Radetzky March*. It is no accident that these two chronicles of loss contain the richest expressions of Roth's preoccupation with the border, the site of crossing from one world into another, of transition and transience, of departure from the familiar into the foreign.

The border is also the place from which the signs of imminent upheaval are most visible. In *The Radetzky March* dwellers in the Austrian border regions perceive the approaching war long before those in Vienna, "not only because they were accustomed to sensing coming things, but also because they could see the portents of collapse every day with their own eyes." Having grown up in a climate of disquiet and ferment that presaged the monarchy's downfall, Roth was keenly aware of the augmented vision of things from the periphery, "where the demise of the world could already clearly be seen, as one sees a storm at the edge of a city, while its streets still lie unsuspectingly and blissfully under a blue sky." This border-perspective is crucial to Roth's world-view as a quintessential outsider, from his beginnings as a fatherless and poetically inclined Jew from Europe's eastern frontier to his last years as an exile in Paris. The acuity of Roth's discernment from the margins is evident in the incisive nature of his journalism, the political foresight of his early fiction, and the emotional profundity of his late work.

The elegiac turn in Roth's writing that begins with *Job* is traceable to the author's afflictions at the time. In 1929 his wife was diagnosed with schizophrenia. Like Deborah Singer in the novel, who is desperate to find a cure for her disabled son, Roth sought the help of a Hassidic rabbi for his stricken wife. The crisis with Friederike must have reawakened the painful memory of his father's madness: Nachum Roth had been entrusted to the custody of a wonder rabbi. The scenes in *Job* in which the Singers' daughter, Miriam, succumbs to insanity and ends up in an asylum reflect the trauma of Friederike's eventual institutionalization. In letters from this period, Roth explained his woes in terms akin to those he uses in *Job*: "It is a curse that has struck me," he wrote, "God alone can help." The novel's fairy-tale ending, in which the rabbi's prophecy comes to pass and father and son are miraculously reunited (and which Roth once confessed he could not have written had he not been drunk), may well have served as a catharsis for the author in more ways than one. The scene in *Job*, in which it is not the father but the son who is healed, is the mirror image of the longed-for reunion that remained an unfulfilled wish outside the realm of fiction. Friederike's psychosis no doubt compounded this grief.

After Hitler's rise to power in 1933, Roth refashioned himself as a Catholic conservative and monarchist. Having fled Berlin for Paris, the writer – who had once signed his articles for socialist-leaning newspapers "Der rote Joseph" (Red Joseph) – espoused the conviction that only the Catholic Church and a resuscitation of Habsburg rule could save Austria and Europe from the Nazi menace. Numerous contemporaries noted Roth's mythomania and his tendency to adopt diverse masks and roles, but this was certainly the most bewildering of his transformations. Still, it seemed to emanate in some way from his elemental yearning for the vanished past, which intensified in those years. At the same time, tormented by guilt over his wife's suffering and burdened by ever-worsening financial strains, Roth – who had always been a heavy drinker – descended ever deeper into the alcoholism that would take his life in 1939. A year later, Friederike would fall victim to the Nazis' so-called "euthanasia" program in an Austrian sanatorium. Roth's art had reached its pinnacle at the point when his life and his world began their tragic collapse.

Ross Benjamin